BILL NYE

& GREGORY MONE

ILLUSTRATED BY
NICK ILUZADA

AMULET BOOKS • NEW YORK

JACK AND THE GENIUSES

LOST IN THE JUNGLE

THE LIBRARY OF CONGRESS HAS CATALOGED THE HARDCOVER EDITION AS FOLLOWS: LIBRARY OF CONGRESS CATALOGING-IN-PUBLICATION DATA NAMES: NYE, BILL, AUTHOR. 1 MONE, GREGORY, AUTHOR. 1 ILUZADA, NICHOLAS, ILLUSTRATOR. TITLE: LOST IN THE JUNGLE / BY BILL NYE & GREGORY MONE : ILLUSTRATED BY NICHOLAS ILUZADA. DESCRIPTION: NEW YORK : AMULET BOOKS, 2018. 1 SERIES: JACK AND THE GENIUSES : 3 1 SUMMARY: WHEN JACK AND HIS GENIUS FOSTER SIBLINGS, AVA AND MATT, DISCOVER INVENTOR HANK WITHERSPOON IS MISSING, THEY TRAVEL DEEP INTO THE AMAZON JUNGLE, OVERCOMING STRANGE CREATURES, A RAGING RIVER, AND SOME VERY CLEVER FOES TO FIND THEIR FRIEND AND PROTECT HIS BIG IDEA. IDENTIFIERS: LCCN 2017057274 1 ISBN 9781419728679 (HARDBACK) SUBJECTS: 1 CYAC: SCIENCE--FICTION. 1 SCIENTISTS--FICTION. 1 RAIN FORESTS--FICTION. 1 AMAZON RIVER REGION--FICTION. 1 GENIUS--FICTION. 1 ORPHANS--FICTION. 1 BROTHERS AND SISTERS--FICTION. 1 ADVENTURE AND ADVENTURERS--FICTION. 1 BISAC: JUVENILE FICTION / SCIENCE & TECHNOLOGY. 1 JUVENILE FICTION / SCIENCE FICTION. 1 JUVENILE FICTION / ACTION & ADVENTURE / GENERAL. CLASSIFICATION: LCC PZ7.1.N94 LO 2018 1 DDC [FIC]--DC23

PAPERBACK ISBN 978-1-4197-3485-4

ABRAMS The Art of Books
195 Broadway, New York, NY 10007
abramsbooks.com

TO ALL THE REAL-WORLD FOSTER CARE
FAMILIES OUT THERE WHO WOULD'VE DONE A
WONDERFUL JOB WITH AVA, JACK, AND MATT.

CONTENTS

1. THE MAN IN THE PURPLE MASK   1

2. AN ELECTRIC IDEA   17

3. NEVER SIT ON AN OSCAR   33

4. THE GRANDMOTHER OF THE IPHONE   60

5. THE BOY WITH THE MILLION-DOLLAR FOOT   72

6. ODORASED   83

7. THE *VON HUMBOLDT*   99

8. HOOKING A MONSTER   111

9. DITCHING THE CAPTAIN   132

10. THE TRAIL OF PAIN   141

11. LASER ASSASSIN   158

12. WHAT HAPPENS IN ASPEN   172

13. AN UNEXPECTED RETURN 186

14. CHERYL TO THE RESCUE 197

15. THE SLOTH LORD 207

16. THE ROOF OF THE
RAINFOREST 214

17. DARKNESS IN THE WATER 221

18. CRIMES AGAINST THE AMAZON 231

19. OUT OF THE DUMPSTER 253

TWELVE MOSTLY ESSENTIAL
QUESTIONS ABOUT *LOST IN THE
JUNGLE* 261

GROWTH IN THE RAINFOREST—
AN EXPERIMENT BY BILL NYE 270

I

THE MAN IN THE PURPLE MASK

THE THREE OF US SPREAD OUT ACROSS THE RUINED lab. When we'd left the night before, the space had been in perfect condition. I'd even swept the floors. But now, early the next morning, the huge room was a disaster. Mechanical birds were lying shattered on the ground. The insides of the self-driving car had been ripped out. Wires spilled from the hood like electronic spaghetti. Even our robotic pizza chef, Harry, was busted. Cables hung down to his wheels. Water was spreading across the floor from a small crack in the twenty-foot-deep submarine test tank.

Across the room, Matt was leaning over a keyboard, scanning a monitor. "Who could have done this?" he asked.

Ava was sitting on the floor, carefully pulling a drone into her lap like it was a bird with a busted wing. "And why?"

Before I could offer a guess, a window exploded high above us.

Glass rained down on the self-driving car. A black cube

bounced off the curved roof of the vehicle and plunked onto the floor. Then it rolled. For a second I thought it might be a grenade. I imagined grabbing the explosive and heroically tossing it high into the air before anyone was hurt. But when it stopped, I realized it was just a camera.

Matt ran over to me and pointed up. The lab was ten stories tall, and the center of the huge space was wide open, but a series of rooms extended out from the walls on platforms. They stretched from the ground floor to the ceiling like spiral stairs, and one of the rooms was puffing out clouds of vapor through a hole in a window. A thin black rope was dangling all the way from the platform to the floor. "Is that the biosphere?" I asked.

"Yes," Matt whispered, "and someone's in there."

"Duh," Ava replied.

"Maybe it's Hank?"

A spark flashed inside the room. A man cursed and shouted.

"That's not Hank," Ava said.

Our friend Hank, otherwise known as Dr. Henry Witherspoon, owns the lab. He lets us work there, too, and takes care of us. Well, sort of, anyway. We hadn't seen or heard from him in three weeks. That was a really long time for him to be gone, especially without sending us a single e-mail or even a quick text. Honestly, I would've settled for an emoji.

But Hank's an unusual guy, and he probably had a great explanation.

Oh, and there's no way he'd wreck his own lab. Especially not the room we were staring up at now. The glass-walled biosphere was one of his favorite spots. About half the size of our apartment, the space was a miniature eco-system, sealed off from the outside world and the rest of the lab. Nothing but light went in or out. The air inside cycled through about twenty different plants and miniature trees, and the water evaporated and condensed as it flowed along a miniature stream that circled the interior. A hidden pump, powered by sunlight, kept the water moving. Sure, the "Do Not Enter" and "Caution" signs were painfully tempting, but not one of us had ever been inside the room.

Not even me.

Honestly.

Except for that one time. Which is kind of how I knew so much about the inside.

Matt grabbed my shirt just above the elbow. "Let's get out of here," he said, still whispering. "Hank would've told us he was back."

This wasn't quite true. Hank showed up and disappeared without warning all the time. But I didn't challenge my brother. I glanced at Ava. She wasn't moving. Matt himself didn't actually look ready to go. But neither of them really wanted to lead the way, either. I'm always the one who goes first. "Fine," I said quietly. "I'll go check it out."

Matt reached over to a small worktable and grabbed a hammer. Ava shot him a look. "Really?" she mouthed.

My brother, who had the muscles of an athlete but the fighting skills of a toddler, deflated like a popped balloon. Hammer or no hammer, he wasn't going to fight anyone. None of us were. He carefully replaced the tool, and we crossed the lab floor as quietly as ninjas.

Now, about this laboratory. It's a little odd. Okay, more than a little. There's a giant water tank for testing submarines and robotic boats and suits that let you stay underwater without air tanks. The glass-encased Mars room is a near-perfect copy of the landscape on the Red Planet. All kinds of vehicles and robots and enough computers to satisfy two classrooms full of kids are scattered around the place. And that's just the ground floor. Each of the platforms that wind up toward the ceiling supports its own miniature lab. The biosphere used to be on the fourth platform, but Hank redesigned it and moved it up a few floors.

The first time Hank let us into his lab, I had no idea how he got from one platform to the next. The giant catapult capable of launching department store mannequins fifty feet in the air suggested he had some exciting plans, but

4

he developed a much easier way up. And the rope dangling from the biosphere's platform suggested that the intruder hadn't found it.

Ava grabbed the rope and gave it a gentle tug. "At least he didn't use Betsy," she said.

Betsy wasn't a kid. Or a pet. My sister liked to name her inventions, and Betsy was a motorized device, about the size of a blender, that let you fire a long cable up to rooftops or balconies and then whisked you right up like Batman. Don't tell her I said that, though, because she hates superheroes. And look, Betsy was amazing. Totally. Even if I had sprained my finger trying to use her the week before. But this wasn't the time for Betsy. We needed to be quiet. And safe.

"I'd rather go the normal way," I said.

Ava flicked a red rubber toggle switch hidden behind a painting of a lighthouse. Two dozen metal steps popped out of the wall with a faint *whoosh*. They weren't connected to each other, only to the wall, and there was no railing, either. Hank had covered each one with a thin square of rubber after Matt had tripped and banged his knees on the metal edges about a dozen times. Naturally, for this reason, I called the squares "Matts." Ava liked the joke. My brother? Not so much.

We hurried up the Matts, and I stopped at the first

5

platform to listen. Whoever was up there in the biosphere wasn't trying very hard to be quiet. Once or twice he shouted another curse . . . but I couldn't quite understand the swear. I flicked the switch for the stairs to the next platform, and we kept moving quietly and carefully, winding clockwise around the interior walls as we ascended. Each platform had its own focus. One was all about growing and harvesting cells. The second was a robotics workshop. Then there was a clean room for experiments that couldn't be contaminated with all the miniature bugs and microbes that crawl around the normal world, a tiny greenhouse, a 3-D printing shop, and, finally, the biosphere.

We stopped on the platform below, outside the 3-D printing room. On the wall next to me was a painful reminder of one of the geniuses' most successful pranks. There was a hook and a hanger and a sign above them that read "Invisibility Cloak." I'm too ashamed to explain. But the supposed cloak wasn't there, anyway, so we'll move on.

Something splashed in the room above. If either my brother or my sister had suddenly decided this whole strategy was a bad idea, and that we should turn back and call for help, I wouldn't have protested. But no one was ready to run, so I reached out and flipped the switch. We waited as the steps *whooshed* out of the walls, then crept up.

The intruder muttered. Then he began to hum a tune.

A pop song. I turned back to my siblings and pointed to one of my ears, hoping they might recognize it. But this was pointless. Neither of them listened to real music. Matt only liked the symphonies of old dead guys, and Ava once told me there was already too much noise in her head to crowd it with tunes. "Never mind," I mouthed.

A sign on the foggy glass read "Do Not Enter!"

I pushed through the swinging door and held it open with my foot. A man wearing a baseball cap and a thin purple ski mask that covered his face below the eyes stared back at me. He was about Hank's height and wearing shorts, a T-shirt, and a dark blue lab coat. His eyes were gray, his eyebrows thin and raised high in surprise. His arms and legs were packed with wiry muscles, and he was wearing an awesome pair of black basketball high-tops. If he hadn't just broken into our lab, I might have complimented him.

He froze.

We froze.

Then he yanked the lab coat up over his head, crouched down with his knees to his chest, and pulled it closed around his legs. Behind me, Ava made a noise. Not a giggle, exactly. But close. Why? Because the intruder had just fallen for the same trick they'd used on me a few weeks before. My siblings are ridiculously smart. Geniuses, really. Ava can build just about anything, and Matt knows more science than

7

Wikipedia. So when I happened to walk past an unfamiliar lab coat hanging on a hook one day, and the sign above it read "Invisibility Cloak," I guessed they'd made another major discovery. How was I supposed to know that it was a joke, and that they were only pretending not to see me as I snuck around the lab the next few days, borrowing various small items I wasn't necessarily supposed to borrow? The whole time they were laughing quietly to themselves. And it wasn't until I tried to grab a few hard candies from Ava's secret drawer that she let me know she could see me.

Now it was my turn. "We can see you," I said. "It's just a coat."

Slowly, the man's head popped out. "I'm not invisible?" he asked.

"Nope, you're not invisible," Ava said. "Who are you? What are you even doing here?"

"And what are you doing to our lab?" Matt added.

"You wrecked everything!" Ava said.

The man stood, then grasped his right arm just below the shoulder. "Where is it?" he asked. His voice was muffled by the mask.

"Where is what?"

"The thumb drive."

"What thumb drive?" Ava asked.

"The one that carries Hank's most important work!"

9

What was he talking about? And what was a thumb drive? The man stepped forward. He glowered. "The police are on their way," I lied. "So you might as well get out of here."

A creature splashed in the artificial river at his back, and the man gripped his arm again. Then he rushed at me. Someday I'm going to be a black belt in one of the martial arts. Jiu-jitsu, maybe. Or kung fu. Whichever one requires the least training. Until then, I'm kind of at a disadvantage, because I have the reaction time of a garden slug. Before I knew what was happening, the man had wrapped me in a headlock. "Where's the thumb drive?" he asked again.

"We really don't know what you're talking about!" Ava yelled back. "Please, let him go."

My brother was strangely quiet. The man clamped down harder on my head. My ears hurt. He yelled at them to back down the stairs as he dragged me out of the room.

"You'll never get out through the front," Matt said. "The police will be here before you even reach the street."

My head was aching, and the intruder definitely didn't wear underarm deodorant. His armpits smelled like pota- toes. "Let me go," I mumbled. He twisted my head again.

"The drive," he said. "Now."

Neither my brother nor my sister responded.

The intruder let go of my head, then stood me upright and gripped the back of my shirt in one hand and the back of my belt in the other. He pushed me forward. I looked out. The ground floor was forty feet down. The no-railing thing really felt like a major design flaw. One easy shove and I was going to sail right off the platform and splatter like a water balloon on the polished concrete.

"Tell me where it is or we'll see if he can fly."

Finally, Matt spoke up. "Hank keeps it with him!"

"Matt!" Ava yelled. "How could you tell him?"

The man loosened his grip on my shirt. But I was still only a half step away from the edge. Trying to break away was too risky. "He keeps it with him?" the intruder asked. He sounded genuinely surprised. "What do you mean?"

"I mean he always has it on him."

"Where is he?"

"We don't know," I said. "Honestly."

Somewhere in the distance we heard sirens.

"They'll be here soon," Matt lied.

The intruder threw me back against the wall, away from the ledge. He hurried back inside the biosphere and slammed the door. Inside, we heard more glass shatter.

Ava yanked the handle. "It's jammed!"

Matt was already dashing down to the next level.

"Don't run away!" Ava called out.

"I'm not," he yelled back.

My sister pulled at the door again.

"Hey," I said, "were you really going to let him push me over the edge?"

She shrugged. "You would've been fine. Hank installed those automatic cushions. The motion sensors would have noticed you as you dropped. That would trigger the cushions to inflate, and then you'd hit one and bounce."

"I'd bounce?"

"Right."

Bouncing off a cushion after a forty-foot drop didn't seem super safe. But I was okay now, and Matt was charging up the stairs with a 3-D printer on his shoulder. Behind my back, I crossed my fingers, hoping he wouldn't trip. Amazingly, he steered his size thirteen sneakers up the steps without a glitch. But why was he carrying the printer in the first place?

Holding the machine just below his right shoulder like a shot put, he rotated to his right, ready to throw.

"Wait!" Ava cried. "Which one is that?"

"It's the Yuko," Matt said.

"Oh, go ahead. That one never works."

Matt hurled the cube at the door, punching a hole in the glass. He reached through and pulled out a metal crowbar that had been jammed through the handle.

Inside, we saw that the window had been kicked out. All three of us leaned through and stared down. The man was running across the roof of the neighboring apartment building. The jump down was maybe eight feet. Another pile of shattered glass was spread out on the blacktopped roof below. The smart move would have been to ask Matt to lower me down carefully. So I planted my foot on the bottom of the opening and leaped.

My heels crunched down on the glass as I landed in a crouch with one hand forward. For a second there, I felt like Iron Man. Only without all the cool gear.

"Jack, what do you think you're doing?" Matt called down.

Think? The lab was our responsibility. One way or another, we had to catch the intruder. So I didn't think. I jumped, and then I ran. Across the roof of the building next door, over a hip-high wall, and onto the next roof a few feet below. Ahead of me, the intruder knocked over an old television antenna and hurdled a chimney like he was a contestant on an obstacle course show. Then he yanked open a rectangular aluminum trapdoor in the roof and, without looking back, dropped through. I heard him curse again. Or at least the way he said it reminded me of a curse. But the word itself sounded foreign.

At the trapdoor, I leaned over the edge and peered through the opening. The intruder had jumped down into a closet stuffed with coats and boxes, but there was a ladder, too. I could hear his hurried footsteps racing down the stairs.

An old lady screamed.

I climbed down the ladder. My foot caught on a fur coat and I tumbled out onto a carpeted landing at the top of two flights of stairs. A cloud of dust puffed up. I sneezed, then hurried to my feet. Leaning over into the stairwell, I could see the intruder's hand grasping the wooden railing as he raced down. The old lady screamed again. The intruder was almost down to the street. The air stank of boiled cabbage and chocolate. Either the residents were cooking up a strange feast or the man had a gas problem.

The old lady was standing in the doorway to her apartment on the second floor, stirring something in a small metal pot. I hurried past her, taking the last flight of the worn wooden stairs three at a time. More clouds of dust and mold rose up as I jumped down onto the carpet at the bottom, and when I burst out onto the sidewalk, I sneezed three more times.

The man was already at the corner.

He was checking his phone, still wearing his ridiculous mask. Was this really a time to text?

I started running. Halfway down the block, Matt and Ava called out from behind me. The man looked up from his phone and broke right. Rounding the corner, I took the

14

turn wide, in case he planned to ambush me, but he was already at the end of the block. I dodged two skinny bearded guys walking toward me with their heads down and earbuds inserted. Clones of the first pair followed, and I squeezed between them just as a large black SUV pulled to a stop at the curb. The man in the purple mask opened the door to the back seat. He ripped off the lab coat and threw it to the sidewalk. I was only twenty feet away. No one stood between us, and for some reason, I yelled, "Stop!"

And he stopped.

This part I hadn't really planned. Slowly, he turned around to face me. The purple mask covered most of his face, but I was certain he was smiling. He held out his left hand, pointed at me with his index finger, and said, "Jack, right?" I was mute. How did he know my name? "You are Jack, aren't you?"

"No," I said. "I'm Ava."

He snickered. My nerves eased. Annoying other people relaxes me.

"I've got a message for your friend Hank," he said.

Matt and Ava caught up and stood on either side of me. "You do?" I asked.

"Yeah," the man said. "If you hear from him, you tell him he can't keep his secret for long. I'll do whatever I have to do to get that drive from him."

15

"You already wrecked his lab," Matt said.

"And knocked some absolutely amazing and totally harmless drones out of the sky!" Ava added.

The man glared at us under the lid of his baseball cap. "Those toys are the least of your problems. If I don't find Hank soon, I'll be back for you three." He stared at each of us in turn, then rested his narrow gaze on me. "And next time we'll see if all of you can fly."

2

AN ELECTRIC IDEA

RIGHT. LET ME BACK UP. I'M JACK, THE CHARMING, daring, and mildly handsome one. I definitely can't fly. I'm pale as a paper towel. My hair is thick and blond. I should have blue eyes, but for some reason they're brown. Sometimes I like to wear bow ties, and if I'm amazing at something, I still haven't found it. But in my search, I've eliminated quite a few athletic endeavors. Basketball and surfing, for example. As for my brains, well, let's just say that in a normal class full of kids my age I might be considered one of the smarter ones. Maybe. But I'm not part of a normal classroom. And I don't hang out with too many kids my age.

Most of the time I'm with my brother and sister. Matt's the oldest. Sometimes he acts like that gives him authority over Ava and me, but we pretty much ignore him when he gets that way. Ava and I are only six months apart. She's taller than I am at this point, but don't tell her I admitted that. Also, the three of us aren't related, exactly, and we look nothing alike. Ava has dark skin and she wears her hair pulled back in a fierce ponytail. Matt has thick, dark hair and a perma-tan. He's tall, too, and his shoulders get wider every week even though he doesn't exercise. Supposedly, Ava was born in Haiti, but Matt and I don't really know where our ancestors originated. Hank would say this doesn't matter at all anyway, because genetically we all trace back to the same people. In one way, we're all from Africa. Or if you want to go back even farther, we're all from the same batch of simple organisms drifting around in the prehistoric soup.

Anyway, the real difference between us doesn't have anything to do with height or color or hairstyle. Hank, Ava, Matt—they're all brilliant. Ava speaks something like eleven languages now. Maybe twelve. As I mentioned earlier, she can build anything. And Matt can pretty much rattle off the entire history of the universe if you ask him, starting with the big bang and rolling forward to the birth of Earth. He's in college. Ava's in high school. She could probably be finished by now, but she says she doesn't want to rush.

Me? I just finished sixth grade.

Kind of depressing, right?

How we ended up together is kind of a long story, so I'll cut it down to the main points. About two years ago, the three of us ended up in the same foster home. There's still some debate about who actually hatched the plan—I vote for me—but at one point, we decided to divorce our foster parents. My brother buried himself in a law school library long enough to master all the relevant legal details, and we convinced a judge to let us live on our own. We're not rich, but we make enough money from our bestselling book of poetry, *The Lonely Orphans*, to support ourselves. And once we began working with Hank—another long story—we started traveling so much that it just didn't make sense to go to a normal school. So now I take my classes online. Sure, I wonder sometimes if it would be better to be in a regular school with regular kids. But regular kids don't get to travel to the South Pole or to private Hawaiian islands. Regular kids don't work in ridiculously cool secret laboratories stocked with wild and weird inventions. And regular kids don't chase masked men out of those secret labs and around city blocks, either. And I kind of like the excitement.

19

All around us, the neighborhood was still waking up. Trucks and taxis and cars of all shapes and sizes were rolling in both directions, but no one was slamming on their horns yet. A bearded man and a blond woman were leaning against a brick wall outside the bodega across the street, eating popsicles. For a second I thought the man was watching us. Or maybe I just wanted his popsicle. The month of August had just jumped up on us, and the heat was pretty horrifying. Luckily, the garbage bags piled along the sidewalks hadn't started to stink yet, and a bagel shop down the block was kicking out some heavenly scents. Smell-wise, this wasn't a bad time of day.

The three of us stood there for a moment and watched the car cruise away. Across the street, part of the way down the block, a police cruiser pulled out from behind a stopped station wagon. That must have been the source of the sirens we'd heard earlier—the cop was probably giving the driver a ticket for speeding. I stepped off the curb, hoping to signal the cruiser, but it turned right, away from the SUV.

"What now?" I asked. "Should we actually call the police?"

"Hank doesn't want anyone in his lab," Ava pointed out. "Not even the police."

We started back toward the lab. Hank's street was quieter, and for a while, no one spoke. I could almost hear their brains working.

"How did he break in?" Ava wondered aloud.

There were two ways into and out of Hank's laboratory. The elevator in the deli across the street was my favorite. The door was hidden in a supply closet in the back, and only Hank and the three of us had the code to operate it. Why did I like that one best? Mostly because Hank had set up a charge account for us, so we could grab a bag of chips or an energy drink on our way in or out, and we didn't even have to pay. But my sister preferred the Dumpster, which rolled away at the press of a button to reveal a hidden set of stairs. That's the way we first snuck into Hank's laboratory a year earlier.

"What about the deli?" Matt suggested.

"He wouldn't know the code," Ava noted. "The Dumpster?"

"No way he could've figured that out," Matt said.

I shrugged. "We figured it out, didn't we?"

"That was mostly me," Matt reminded us.

Ava started to reply, then stopped herself and hurried ahead. Back inside the lab, the puddle was growing. Ava rushed off to open the drains in the tank to prevent the whole room from being flooded.

"What now?" I asked.

"Clues," Matt said. "Look around for anything that might tell us who this guy is, and why he was here."

The tank began emptying, and Ava returned.

"He had pretty sweet high-tops," I said.

Staring at the ceiling, Ava started tapping her foot. "And that weird purple mask," she said. "Plus he's gullible enough to believe we developed an invisibility cloak."

"Plenty of smart people could've fallen for that," I said. "What was he looking for? What's this drive he was talking about?"

21

"The thumb drive?" my brother asked.

"Right," I said. I was picturing a little robotic thumb that could jump off your hand and drive around. Maybe it would have a camera. Or it could go into a bathroom ahead of you to see if the air stinks from one of your brother's recent battles.

"It's basically a memory stick," Matt said.

That didn't help much.

"It's a little disk about the size of your thumb," Ava said. "You can store files, photos, documents. Anything you'd store on a computer, really."

"And Hank uses one?"

My sister nodded. "I don't know why, but he started storing all his work on this one little drive and carrying it with him everywhere."

"Is that why he started wearing the fanny pack?" I asked.

Lately, the few times we'd seen him, Hank had been wearing a small pack with a belt that clipped around his waist. We were always trying to convince him to ditch it, because he looked like a tourist. He refused.

"No," Ava said. "The thumb drive can fit in your pocket. I still don't know why he wears that fanny pack." She slumped down and sat on the rubber track that looped around the room. Then she leaned back against the self-driving car. "I don't get it," she said. "What was Hank working on? What

22

was so important that someone would break into the lab?"

Our mentor was always busy. He traveled at least a few times a month to faraway cities and countries for meetings and conferences. Normally, he'd check in with us to ask what we were working on and whether we needed anything—or to find out if I'd accidentally set off an explosion that turned the lab into rubble. He'd tell Matt and Ava about his latest projects, too. He seemed to enjoy sharing his ideas with them. But lately he'd been different. Quiet. Secretive. Instead of traveling for a few days, he'd be gone for weeks. Sure, we survived. We were used to being on our own. But this was different, and I don't think any of us really liked it. No one said it quite this way, exactly, but we felt abandoned.

"Maybe it was some kind of military project," Matt suggested. "A new weapon or something."

Ava shook her head. "No. Hank says the world has enough weapons."

"Aliens?" I suggested.

"What?"

They were staring at me like I was an alien. "Yeah, I mean you guys were doing all that satellite work, and Hank's always talking about intelligent life on other worlds. Maybe he finally made contact and he's been teleporting to some far-off planet and learning about their culture and getting ready to introduce them to Earth." I wanted to call them

23

Zorbakians. And I wanted them to be green and one eyed, with tiny little hands the size of donut holes. Ideally, they'd make little high-pitched noises when they tried to communicate, and they'd be amazing but funny dancers. The kind of dancers you can laugh and point at without hurting their feelings.

"Are you really asking if he discovered aliens?" Matt asked.

"Stop," Ava said. "We're getting off track."

As she said it, she stood and stepped off the track. I laughed and pointed. She closed her eyes and shook her head, and then we started back up the Matts to the biosphere. Along the way, my brother pointed out that the intruder didn't do anything to the other stations. Each one was untouched. Yet the biosphere was ruined. Inside, the pump that kept the artificial river moving had stopped working. As Matt reached in to get it operating again, a small eel writhed near the surface. I reached forward to pet the weird, slimy little dude.

At the last second, Ava grabbed my wrist. "Careful," she said, "that's electric."

"Maybe that's why he was holding his shoulder," Matt guessed. "Do you think he got shocked?"

"If he was stupid enough to pet an electric eel," Ava said.

That stung a little. Matt glanced at me, but she didn't see the connection. I moved on. "Why this room?" I asked. "Why the biosphere?"

"It's basically a model rainforest," Matt explained.

"People are always looking for new medicines down in the rainforest," Ava said. "Maybe Hank found something."

A door slammed below us. Matt grabbed my shoulder as a woman called out in a familiar voice, "Hello? Hank?"

All three of us hurried out of the room and looked down. "Min," Ava said. "What's she doing here?"

At one point, Min was kind of our handler, appointed by Social Services to look after us and make sure we really were capable of taking care of ourselves. Or that was her job a while ago, anyway. Then we went missing out in the Hawaiian Islands, and she flew out to help Hank track us down, and pretty soon after that she wasn't working for Social Services anymore. Now I'm not sure what she does, but she still checks in on us, and she spends a suspicious percentage of her time with Hank. But we'd never actually seen Min in the lab. I didn't even know she knew how to get inside.

Ava hurried to see her first. Matt adjusted something

else on the pump, and the river started flowing again. After another glance at the wriggling eel, I followed him down.

Min pushed her glasses up on top of her head. "What happened?" she asked.

"Someone broke in."

"Are you okay? Were any of you hurt?"

My head still ached a little. "I kind of—"

"We're fine," Ava answered.

Then we told her everything. She nodded along as she listened.

"Have you heard from Hank?" Ava asked.

"Not for three weeks. I came here to look for him."

"Do you know where he's been?"

"No."

"Did you notice anything different about him?" Matt asked.

"Besides how weird he's been acting," Ava added.

"Like I said, I haven't heard from him for three weeks. He hasn't replied to any of my calls or e-mails. That's very unusual."

"Anything else?" I asked.

Min thought for a moment. "Archery," she said.

"You mean like bows and arrows?"

She nodded. "Yes. We went to an archery range together. He was very impressive."

Ava snapped her fingers. "I just thought of one more thing. He might have taken up smoking."

"Smoking? No," Min insisted. "That's impossible. Why would you think that?"

Ava rushed off to the bathroom, then returned with a book of matches. "Then how do you explain these?" she asked.

Nobody knows everything. That's impossible. But sometimes it feels like my siblings do know everything, so when one of them suddenly reveals a tiny gap in their knowledge of the universe, I'm thrilled. Delighted. Ecstatic, to borrow one of Hank's favorite words. So when I realized Ava didn't know why there were matches in the bathroom, I laughed. And so did Min.

"What?" Matt asked. "I don't get it."

This was getting even better. "The matches are for odors . . . you know? In the bathroom?"

The longest and most wonderful three seconds of my short life followed before they understood. During that stretched-out instant, I was the smart one, the one who knew that something in the smoke from a recently lit match floats up into your nose and overpowers the scent of whatever disaster the previous person dropped into the bowl, smothering those stink particles. I knew that. They didn't.

For three seconds, anyway.

27

"Oh," Matt said.

"Oh!" Ava added.

"Let me see those," Min requested. Ava tossed her the matchbook. She studied the cover. "Saudade? I don't know this restaurant. Has he taken you there?"

"No," I answered.

Ava was typing on her phone. She waited, then turned her head slightly as the results of her search popped up. "It's not in New York. It's not even in this country." She turned the phone and showed us the screen. "The restaurant is in Brazil."

Immediately Matt glanced up at the biosphere. "That matches up with his interest in the rainforest," he said. "Brazil is home to the biggest section of the Amazon rainforest, one of the most diverse and unique ecosystems in the world. I heard once that a new species is discovered every three days in the Amazon. That's where most electric eels live, too. They're much bigger than the little one upstairs."

Ava tapped her screen. "The restaurant is in Manaus," she added. "A city known as the gateway to the Amazon."

"So Hank's in Brazil?" I asked.

No one answered at first.

"Maybe," Matt concluded.

"Why?" Ava asked. "What's he working on?"

"Whatever it is, it's big enough for someone to break in here," Matt said.

28

"And almost kill me," I reminded them.

"What?!" Min asked.

Ava rolled her eyes. "He would have been fine."

Min was checking me over. I decided to tell her all about it later. At least she might offer a little sympathy.

"Maybe we missed something upstairs," Matt said.

He started back up, and he wasn't even to the second landing when it struck me. "The eel!"

All three of them responded with some variation of "Huh?"

Okay. A quick little rewind here. A lot of ideas flow through Hank's laboratory. Hank himself is responsible for most of them, of course. But my siblings are crazy productive, too. Most recently, Ava and Matt had designed their own CubeSat—a miniature satellite about the size of a toaster. They named the device Cheryl, and it had some amazing capabilities. Cheryl could take photos, send and receive data, and more. Launching her into space wasn't easy, but Hank had made plans to send up a pair of satellites of his own. One of them failed, so I kind of sent a few notes to the rocket company from his e-mail account and convinced them to launch Cheryl instead.

A few weeks later, the rocket soared up through the atmosphere, dropping Cheryl into orbit. She'd been whipping around the globe ever since, and the geniuses had been spending most of their time tracking and programming her.

29

The whole project was supposed to be a surprise for Hank, but they hadn't gotten the chance to tell him yet. Which I didn't mind, because when he did find out, I'd have to explain the whole e-mail thing.

As for me, the ideas don't flow out quite so fast. They trickle. But occasionally I'm struck with brain lightning, too. Almost nine months ago, we were on the remote Hawaiian island of Nihoa, dealing with a bazillionaire, an air-conditioning king, and a brilliant engineer. Long story. Anyway, I had this idea. Someone had been talking about energy, and the subject of electric eels came up, and I kind of blurted out that it might be cool to use them to power a house or even a car. Everyone laughed at me. Well, everyone except Hank. He said he thought there might be something to the notion. And that was it.

But now he'd been spending time in Brazil, near the heart of the Amazon. Matt himself had just said that the Amazon was home to most of the world's electric eels. Hank had rebuilt the biosphere and stocked it with an electric eel. And someone had just broken into our lab and taken apart both that room and the electric self-driving car.

What if he was looking for eels inside?

I hurried over to inspect the engine up close.

"What are you doing?" Ava asked.

I explained.

This time Min laughed.

"Come on, Jack," Matt said. "This is serious."

"You can't power a car with electric eels," Ava said.

Matt's expression changed. He held his hand to his chin and glanced back up at the biosphere. "No, but . . ."

In a near whisper, staring at my brother, Ava said, "You could learn from them." She glanced at the car, then the biosphere. "Biomimicry?"

"What's that?" Min asked.

"I know!" I shouted.

"You don't have to raise your hand, Jack," Min said. "What is it?"

"When inventors or engineers borrow tricks from nature. They study how a plant or insect or bird does something and then try to copy the idea in a machine."

31

"Maybe he's been studying the way eels shock their prey to invent some new weapon or something," Matt guessed.

"Or a better battery," I suggested.

Ava pointed to the car. "One that could power an electric vehicle?"

"People would pay millions for a better battery," Matt said.

Min corrected him. "Try hundreds of millions."

I pulled out my phone and started searching.

"Jack," Min said, "what are you doing?"

"I'm looking up flights."

"Flights to where?"

I figured that was obvious. "Hank's in trouble, guys," I said. "We have to warn him, but we have to find him first, and all the evidence points to one place. We're going to Brazil."

3

NEVER SIT ON AN OSCAR

FIVE DAYS LATER WE WERE IN THE AIR, FLYING SOUTH. Min wasn't able to come with us, but she begged us to send her constant updates. Also, Matt bought us the worst tickets possible. I don't want to sound too spoiled or anything, but we'd once ridden in a private jet belonging to J. F. Clutterbuck, the billionaire inventor of the odorless sock. Once you experience that level of living, a normal plane is pretty disappointing. The soda doesn't even taste as sweet. And we had to ride on four normal planes. There were nonstop flights, but my brother said they were too expensive. So we flew to Chicago first, then Charlotte. We waited there for six hours. Next was Miami, where we had to wait another five hours before finally flying south to Manaus, the unofficial capital of the Amazon.

Before the trip, everything I'd known about Brazil came from some animated movies about a bunch of talking birds. So I needed to educate myself. I packed a few books from the library, grabbed a few more from this little bookstore around the corner from our apartment, and downloaded a bunch of documentaries, along with a movie called *Monkey Boy*, about a kid who crashes in the Amazon jungle. Matt told me it was silly and juvenile, but he totally watched it over my shoulder. He'd secretly watched a bunch of movies I'd recommended recently, including a trilogy called *Sniper Assassin*. Those were really cool, though. The sniper was so good that when people noticed the little red dot from his laser sight on their chests, they just gave up right away, and he didn't even have to pull the trigger.

Anyway, on our final flight, strengthened by a few cups of milky, sugary coffee delivered in little Styrofoam cups and at least a dozen of these golf-ball-size gummy cheese rolls called *pão de queijo*, I devoured as much information about Brazil as I could. Ava was learning Portuguese through a language app on her phone, and Matt was fiddling with the computer code that controlled Cheryl, their satellite. They were busy. So if I studied hard, I could be our expert on Brazil. I carry a pocket-size notebook with me most of the time, so I opened that up and jotted down cool facts as I read.

First of all, Brazil is huge—as large as the United States, not counting Alaska. Two hundred million people live down there, and there's definitely more to it than soccer and samba. The country was colonized by the Portuguese in the sixteenth century, and Hank wasn't the first person to study its electric eels. A visiting German scientist named Alexander von Humboldt once drove forty horses into eel-infested waters to see what would happen. The eels jolted the poor beasts, and a bunch of them died. The only good part of the story is that Von Humboldt kept experimenting, shocking himself so frequently that he was sick for days.

Today, Brazil is stocked with resources like oil and natural gas, and the Brazilian people spend more on beauty products than anyone else in the world. Even poor folks can get plastic surgery. Apparently they're close talkers in Brazil, too, and very fond of hugs. Ava wasn't going to like that. As for soccer, well, it's more than a sport in Brazil. It's more like a religion. Players and fans sob when they lose. They cry when they win.

But we're not going to that Brazil. Or not exactly, anyway. If Hank was off studying electric eels, then he was probably somewhere deep in the Amazon rainforest, and that was a world of its own. Before we left, I was looking forward to the trip. Hiking, sleeping in hammocks, watching cool monkeys swing from trees, laughing as my brother tripped over hidden roots and face-planted in the jungle. There was a chance I'd see one of my favorite animals, the sloth, up close. It sounded like the perfect vacation. But the more I read, the more that changed. Before long, I was petrified.

The Amazon jungle is one of the most dangerous places on Earth. The river is stocked with alligator-like monsters called caimans, sharp-toothed piranhas, and candiru, menacing little fish that can swim up into your body if you pee in the water. The jungle itself is so thick in places that you have to hack yourself a path with a kind of sword called a "machete." Okay, so maybe that part sounded kind of fun, but now imagine you're doing that in the dark. In some spots, the tall trees form a roof over your head that blocks out almost all the light.

Jaguars roam the forest floors. They swim, too, so you can't even ditch them by jumping into the river and hoping you dodge the piranhas. Vampire bats might swoop down at night and sink their teeth into you when you're sleeping. There are bugs that bite your lips. Bugs that burrow under your skin like it's a sleeping bag. Bugs that make you go blind twenty years after they bite you. Bugs that squirt deadly chemicals. Even the ants are terrifying. One species is known to chew through the walls of your tent. Some shred your underpants.

So, yeah. Not exactly a vacation spot.

Four hours into the last flight, seated next to two snoring women with hair that smelled like potpourri, I started to panic. Forget the hammock and the funny monkeys. Now I was picturing myself racing through the jungle, half-blind and covered with bug bites, my underpants shredded by ants, and my entire soul wishing we'd just stayed home in Brooklyn. I shut the last of the books and sat back. My row mate's hair spray was really bothering me, and I was considering testing out a device I'd grabbed from the lab before we left. The little beauty was about the size of a small tube of toothpaste, and it was inspired by the nose vacuum, one of Hank's greatest inventions. Basically, it sucked up unpleasant smells the way the nose vacuum cleaned up boogers. Hank called it "the Odoraser," and I'd never actually tried it out. So I pretended to reach for the reading lamp over my head, held it above the woman's hair, and sucked in the scent.

For a few minutes, at least, the air was breathable.

The man seated across the aisle from me reached over and tapped the cover of the book on the top of my stack, *Surviving the Amazon*. The lights in the plane were dim. I couldn't see him clearly, but he had very round eyes and a short beard. "The Amazon; it's not so bad," he said.

"No?" I looked down at the stack of books, then back at him. "It seems terrifying."

He waved his hands dismissively. "Don't believe all that," he said. "If you go, just find a good guide and do what he or she says." The man reached down into the bag below the seat

37

in front of him. "Oh, and wear these at night," he added, handing me a small pouch. "I carry them with me for long flights, but I cannot sleep. You take them."

I opened the pouch. "Earplugs?"

"Trust me. You'll need them."

We finally landed in the late afternoon, and we limped off the plane like we'd just flown back from Venus. All the airport signs were in Portuguese, and Matt nearly tricked me into walking into the women's bathroom. When we picked up our bags, it took us three hours to convince the security officials to let us through. Three kids traveling to a different country all on their own is strange enough, I guess, but when you peek into their suitcases and find that the gadgets outnumber the clothes, questions are asked. Thankfully, Ava had learned enough Portuguese on the plane to convince them that we weren't smugglers or criminals.

Outside the terminal, the air was warm and wet. A thin rain was falling. Taxis and cars cruised past. Some were parked at an angle, some parallel. A van drove right up onto the sidewalk to pick up a lady with huge sunglasses and long black hair. Matt had his hand to his forehead, staring back into the traffic at a big, white, rusted rectangular vehicle spewing gray smoke. "There's our bus," he said.

"Our bus?"

"We're not taking the bus," Ava said.

38

My sister and I didn't always agree, but this time I was with her. She waved to a passing taxi. The driver screeched to a stop and roared into reverse, forcing several oncoming cars to swerve out of the way. He leaned through the passenger window. "*Onde você vai?*"

"He wants to know where we're going," Ava said.

"Taxis are too expensive," Matt snapped.

Ava and I jumped in anyway. Matt grunted and followed us, forcing me into the middle seat.

I hate the middle seat.

The ride to the city might have been interesting. The driver spoke a little English, and he played tour guide, pointing at buildings and hills and telling stories. He was talking about the famous Amazon Theatre, an opera house built by the fabulously wealthy citizens of Manaus in the nineteenth century, when I fell asleep. The next time my eyes opened, a thick string of drool hung from the corner of my mouth and my stomach felt like it had been stuffed with gravel. Eating a dozen of those cheese bread puffs was not a good idea. A series of unpleasant smells was trying to escape from my body, but I sucked each one up with the Odoraser before they could knock out one of my siblings.

The driver said we were turning onto Avenida Alberto Santos-Dumont. "The street is named after the Brazilian who invented flight," he explained.

39

"The Wright brothers invented flight," Matt insisted.

"No," the driver countered. "Santos-Dumont was first."

I elbowed my brother. "We're in his country," I reminded him. "There's no point arguing."

A few minutes later, the car slammed to a stop.

Rain was splashing off the hood. "I thought this was the dry season," Ava said.

The driver laughed. "The dry season is still wet," he said. "Just a little less wet."

When my brother had said he'd booked us rooms at a great hotel, I pictured chandeliers and marble floors. Clerks in tuxedos. Silk sheets on the beds and ultra-fast Wi-Fi in the rooms. Maybe one of those pitchers with lemon and cucumber water. But our hotel looked abandoned. The sidewalk in front was cracked and buckled in so many places that I had to zigzag just to get to the stone front steps. They were partially busted, too, and a dented silver bowl filled with muddy water sat to one side. Hopefully that wasn't the hotel's idea of free drinks.

Ava and I grabbed the bags, and after paying our driver, Matt hurried past us to the front desk. The clerk wore a yellow and green soccer jersey. An unlit cigarette hung from his lips. Matt started arguing with him, and after a few minutes, Ava got up to help. She listened to the clerk, then turned to Matt. "He says the card was declined."

"Ask him to try again."

She did, but the result was the same, and Matt's face was turning red. He tried four different cards—I didn't even know we had that many—before one finally worked, and then he sighed so dramatically that you would've thought he'd just been proven innocent of a crime. He handed me a key and grabbed his bags.

"What was that all about?" I asked.

"Nothing," Matt snapped.

Our room was fine. Okay, I guess. The shower was clean, anyway. I dropped back onto the bed and was ready to test it for about fourteen hours, but a balled-up pair of socks bounced off my forehead.

"Come on," my brother said. "We're only a few blocks from Saudade, the restaurant. We might as well get started."

41

I sat up, yawned, and stretched. He was right. But I was exhausted. "Can't we wait until tomorrow? And were those socks even clean?"

"No and no."

Ava stood next to Matt. "Come on, Jack. Do we need to remind you that Hank is in danger?"

"Potentially in danger," I noted.

"Potential and actual are only the slightest nudge apart."

"Huh?"

"Just get up."

Thankfully, they allowed me a few minutes to change. My T-shirt smelled like hair spray. Plus, Saudade was a five-star restaurant. This was serious business. I pulled out a short-sleeved button-down shirt, jeans, black high-tops, and a bow tie printed with tiny piranhas. (I may have done a little shopping before we left.) Matt kept yelling at me to hurry up, and Ava wondered how many times I was planning on retying my bow tie. "Until it's perfect," I answered.

That required four attempts. After grabbing a waterproof jacket and briefly adjusting my hair, I followed my siblings out into the city. The rain had slowed, but only slightly, and the sidewalk was cracked and busted for blocks. Cars and taxis dodged and weaved around the potholes scattered across the street. Matt had memorized the route, and he led us onto a block crowded with restaurants and juice bars serving smoothies and puddings packed with the wonder berries of the Amazon, a little fruit called "açaí." The windows were all closed and steamy from the heat and the rain. I was trying to peek inside one spot when my sister grabbed my arm. "Watch it!" she warned.

A pack of kids who had to be a few years younger than Ava and me swarmed past us, all smiles and laughter. They were dressed in tattered T-shirts and tank tops and wore plain sandals on their feet. One kid pointed at my tie, then made a chomping motion. Imitating a piranha, I guessed.

A few of them offered me high fives. Naturally, I accepted, and soon I was high-fiving the whole bunch of them. Matt and Ava were reluctant at first, but they joined in, too. I felt like a pop star, and by the time the kids had raced down the street and around the corner, my siblings were beaming, too.

"That was so cool!" Ava said.

Matt shook his head. "You'd never see kids in New York do that. Right?"

I shrugged. "I have a way with people."

Saudade, the restaurant, was only a few doors down, and the rain slowed as we approached. The front was pure, clean green, as if someone had painted it just the day before. A huge square window, miraculously free of fog, allowed a decent view of the inside. "It looks crowded," I said.

Inside, a woman with long and oddly straight black hair greeted us with a smile. A few dozen matchbooks were stacked neatly in a glass tray. They were exactly like the one we'd found in the lab.

Ava spoke briefly in Portuguese before the woman held up a finger and walked to the back of the restaurant, toward the kitchen. "Where's she going?"

"To get the manager, I think," Ava answered.

Not a single table was empty, but we weren't really there to eat, anyway. Three thin wooden chairs were lined up

43

against the wall behind us. I yawned. I started to sit down when a man called out to me from across the room. "No, no, no! Not my Oscars!"

A few dozen diners turned to face me. I stood straight and held up my hands. "Sorry. What?"

The man was in his fifties and wearing a white apron stained brown and red and purple. His hair was a mix of gray and charcoal, his thick beard nearly white. His brown eyes looked almost too big for someone his size, and he had the thick forearms of a construction worker, not a chef. Still, his huge smile and large eyes somehow made him less frightening. "No, no, please, I'm sorry!" He held his palms out, toward me. "But you must understand, you cannot sit in my Oscars."

"Your Oscars?"

"The chairs. Designed by Oscar Niemeyer—"

"The architect," Matt said. "He designed Brasilia, the capital city, right?"

"Yes, yes! You know architecture?"

"They know everything," I said. So much for me being the expert on the country.

The man eyed me and scratched his bearded chin with a calloused finger. The sound was like a scrub brush digging into a dirty pan.

"You," he said, pointing to me. "I like your tie."

"Thank you."

"I know you," he continued. "From where?"

Matt reached forward and shook the man's hand. "We wrote *The Lonely Orphans*," he said. "It was just published in Brazil last year. The sales haven't been as great as—"

"Orphans? Why are you talking about orphans? I don't know about these orphans. But you," he said, pointing at me with his thumb, "who are you?"

Adjusting my hair, tweaking my bow tie, I replied, "I'm Jack. This is Ava. He's Matt. Are you the owner?"

"Ah, yes, of course. Joaquim Andres da Silva Ribeiro. Chef and owner."

"That's a lot of names."

"In Brazil we like names. My brother has eleven names. But we just call him Boo."

45

I laughed. Matt kicked me.

"It's okay," Joaquim said. "It's funny."

"Do you have a business card?" I asked.

Matt sighed. "Not now, Jack."

A few months earlier, I'd started collecting business cards. Asking for them was probably the best part. It made me feel official. Grown up.

Joaquim passed me a clean card printed on fine green paper. I slipped it in my pocket as he grabbed a tablet from the desk. "Do you have a reservation?"

"Actually, we're not here to eat," Ava said.

"This is a restaurant. This is why people come here. To eat."

"We're hoping you could help us find a friend of ours," Ava explained. "He was here recently."

"Recently? You mean like yesterday?"

"Sometime in the last few months."

Joaquim winced and breathed in through his teeth. "We serve one hundred people every day. Thousands have eaten here in the past few months."

"I could show you a picture," Ava suggested. She patted her pockets. Then she looked at me. "My phone. I don't have my phone."

Matt searched through his pockets, too. "Mine's gone."

Now they were both looking at me. I shrugged. "I didn't do it. And I left mine in my room."

"Did you walk here?" Joaquim asked.

Matt nodded. "Yes. Why?"

"And maybe along the way you bumped into some cute and friendly kids about your age?"

"We did," I said. "They were so nice! I feel like we really made a connection."

The chef shrugged. "They have your phones."

For a few seconds, none of us spoke. I don't know about the other two, but I was silently replaying the scene in my head. The high fives. They totally pickpocketed us during the high-fives.

"Seriously?" Ava asked. "They stole our phones? I'm calling the police."

Joaquim suggested this was not worth our time. "You have your wallets?" he asked. I had mine; Matt and Ava both nodded as well. "Good. See? These boys are not so bad. They leave your wallets. And you will be fine, so there is no use calling the police. They could say that you committed a crime by not being more careful with your devices. Still, I understand your problem. Now you do not have a picture of your friend."

My sister said something in Portuguese. He handed her the tablet. She searched online, found a photo of Hank, and showed it to him. Joaquim studied the image for a few seconds before apologizing with a shrug. But Ava wasn't giving up. She pointed to the cameras in each of the four corners of the room. "Can we look through your security footage to see if he was here?"

The chef folded his arms across his chest and tilted his head. He breathed deep several times and watched each of us through partially closed eyes. "Why is this so important? Who is this man?"

"He is very famous," I said.

Joaquim laid his arm across my shoulders and pointed

47

back into the room. "There is the mayor of Manaus," he said, pointing to a woman with short gray hair. "The woman next to her is one of the most powerful businesspeople in all of Brazil." He pointed to the next table. "That man was once one of the best football players in the world. The famous and powerful dine here every night."

"His name is Dr. Henry Witherspoon," Matt said. "But we call him Hank."

Nothing.

"Inventor of the nose vacuum?" I added.

Still Joaquim had no clue.

Ava rattled off a dozen of Hank's best-known inventions.

Joaquim told her to stop. "I don't want to know about these accomplishments. Why are you looking for him? Is he your friend? Your uncle? Your father?"

None of us answered. I looked to Matt. But he was waiting for Ava to explain it. Finally, I said, "That's a tough question."

"Not really," Joaquim said.

"He's not our dad," Ava said.

"No?"

"Not exactly," I said.

"Yes or no."

I didn't want to answer. Neither did my siblings. "Look," I said, "we just really need to find him, okay? Can we please scan the footage?"

"Please?" Ava added.

Joaquim quickly sucked air in through his nose, then replied. "No."

"Please?" Matt asked.

"No."

So I was almost thirteen years old. My pouting face should have been retired permanently. But we needed to see that video. We needed this guy's sympathy. We needed him to really, truly feel for us. So I tilted my head forward and down. I raised my lower lip. Then I tried to remember how I'd felt before I met Ava and Matt. I conjured a few of my worst memories, all those first moments in a new foster home, when I had no idea what to expect. Or the nights I'd lie in my bed in our apartment, wondering what it would be like if I had a parent to tuck me in or even just lean through the doorway and wish me sweet dreams. My jaw tingled. My vision blurred as tears formed around my eyes. The first drops raced down my cheeks. And then I fluttered my long eyelashes.

Suddenly, Joaquim's expression changed. "Yes! Yes! I do know you! I know this face!"

This was not the reaction I'd expected.

"You know him?" Matt asked.

The chef reached forward and grabbed my face in his hands. He wiped the tears from my eyes with his huge thumbs. His fingers smelled like salt and spices. Then he shook my head a few times, gently, before letting go. "The video! The puppy . . . You are the boy who gave CPR to that adorable dog!" Holding his hands in the prayer position, he spun to face the kitchen and yelled something in Portuguese. Several cooks came rushing toward us.

Now, about the puppy. There's this video out there of yours truly giving CPR to a very adorable little dog. The moment when I turn my pouting face to the camera with tears in my eyes is definitely stirring. The video is insanely popular, too—nearing sixteen million views the last time I checked. But it's also just a tiny bit fake. The little guy wasn't really unconscious. We concocted the idea while we were in the middle of the court case. My brother was trying to argue that we didn't need foster parents, and that we could take care of ourselves, and we figured the puppy video would sway people to our side and show them that we had heart, too. Matt and Ava insist that his legal argument won the case, but I have to believe the puppy played a role, too. Still, I'd never met any fans of the video in person before.

Joaquim swung his arms around the shoulders of two of his smiling chefs and explained. "Every day we watch this video, as a staff, to remind ourselves that there is good in the world, that the people we serve could be capable of this kindness. Our mission is to honor every diner as if he or she were the magnificent boy in that video. And now . . . this boy is here! In my restaurant. Please, you will eat. You must eat. I will find you a table."

Joaquim twirled, surveyed the dining room, and marched to a group of four. Two men and two women sat below a painting of a monstrous, scaly fish. One of the women was steering a reddish chunk of steak toward her open mouth with a bright silver fork when Joaquim grabbed her plate. Next he grabbed her neighbor's dish. He called to a waitress. She rushed over and took the other two plates of food. The woman with the steak jumped to her feet and began yelling at Joaquim. He shouted back.

"Can you tell what they're saying?" I asked.

"I haven't learned insults yet," Ava said. "But I think she said something about a capybara."

"A huge rodent common in the jungle," Matt explained. "Great swimmers."

I knew that. They kind of looked like mutant groundhogs.

"You think he's kicking them out for us?" Ava asked.

The two men glared at me.

"Looks that way," I said.

The woman yelled another insult, and Joaquim pressed his fists against his eyes and began to cry. Then the woman started to sob, too. A moment later, they hugged.

"What's happening?" I asked.

"I have no idea," Ava said.

"Fascinating," Matt remarked, watching them. He reminded me of Hank when he said it, but he didn't need to hear that.

The waitress led the four diners into the kitchen, and Joaquim called us over as he cleared the table. A waiter quickly laid down clean plates and silverware. Joaquim followed my stare toward the kitchen. "You are worried about them? Do not worry. She is my sister. She eats here once a week. They can finish their food in the kitchen. No problem."

Later, I'd have to ask him for that capybara insult. Matt deserved that one now and then. My brother leaned over the table, studying the menu. He leaned toward Ava and whispered, "I'm not sure we can afford—"

"Afford? You will not pay." Joaquim clapped me on the back so hard my heart did a double beat. "Please. Sit. Order. Eat."

Matt and I slid into the chairs, but Ava remained standing. "What about the security videos?"

"You can watch them later."

"I'd like to get started now."

Joaquim scratched his chin. He watched Ava through narrowed eyes, and she stared back, clear and strong, as if some kind of light were shining from deep inside her brain. The chef's stern expression changed slowly into a smile as he gave in to my sister's demand. "I'll show you the way," he said.

"Order me something basic, like pasta," Ava called back.

Matt called the waiter and asked for an English menu, but there wasn't one. So my brother suggested they bring us cheeseburgers. Plus some pasta. The waiter smiled. I didn't like his smile.

"Why would Hank eat here?" Matt asked.

"Because he was hungry?"

"Ha. Very funny. I mean, why this place? He's vegetarian now, right?" My brother nodded to a neighboring table. The plates were stacked with juicy steaks and pork. "Looks like everything in here is for carnivores."

"Maybe someone invited him here."

"Who?"

"Hopefully Ava will find out."

When the food arrived, I nearly jumped out of my seat. The waiter smiled again and said something in Portuguese. On the plates he set down in front of us, four large cubes of yellow-orange mangoes sat in a brownish purple sauce. And perched atop each mango was a large black ant. I gently poked one with my fork. Thankfully, it was dead.

"Did you think it was going to run? They're not alive," Matt said. "Insects are a great source of protein."

"Then you eat one."

He paled. I knocked one of my ants off its fruity perch, pushed the mango around in the sauce, and devoured it. Matt watched me. "It's delicious," I said. "Honestly."

"You like my tucupi?"

Joaquim stood over us. "Tucupi?" I asked.

"The sauce. I add ground-up ants. Very complex flavors."

Ava squeezed by him. "Where's my pasta?" she asked.

"They serve ants here."

She shrugged. "Oh, well. Good source of protein." Then she forked one of the little creatures and its mango and chomped away. "Not bad. Kind of lemony."

I was supposed to be the adventurous one. The risk-taker. Couldn't she just let me have that? Even if it meant I had to eat ants?

"How'd it go? Did you find anything?"

Ava finished chewing. "We should get a hit within the hour."

"A hit?"

"I downloaded a software program that analyzes videos for faces, then I gave it a few pictures of Hank, so it knows what to look for. The search should take about an hour."

"Nice," Matt said.

"And it'll find Hank?"

"If he's in those videos, it should," Ava said. "Hank and about a hundred other people, probably." She crunched down another ant. "The program captures still pictures from the videos. It'll be easier for us to pick him out of a hundred or so pictures than months' worth of video."

Joaquim returned and pointed to my plate. I was the only one who hadn't tried one of the little crawlers. "Jack?"

I scooped one up, closed my eyes, and crunched away. Ava was right. The taste kind of reminded me of Thai food. The back of the ant popped in my mouth like a ripe grape. "Definitely lemony."

Our host beamed. "Good! You tried my ants. Now I will bring you pasta and hamburgers."

Later, after we'd each wolfed down a bowl of spaghetti and one of the most delicious burgers ever, Ava checked the back office, then returned with a piece of paper in her hand and a smile on her face. "Got him," she said, laying the printout on the table.

Our waiters returned with some kind of pineapple-based dessert that looked absolutely amazing. But it would have to wait. I leaned forward. The photo was slightly blurry, but there was no doubt it was Hank. He was seated at a table with two kids, a boy and a girl. The boy looked to be about my age, and his left foot was propped on the table and wrapped

55

in some kind of cloth or towel. The girl might have been Matt's age or maybe a little younger. Her eyes were wide, her face round, and her hair short and straight and dark.

"Who are they?" I asked.

"And why is Hank letting that kid eat with his foot on the table?" Matt asked. "He'd never let me do that."

Hands on her head, eyes squinted, Ava was straight-up confused. Me? I just felt kind of cheated. What was Hank doing with those two kids? We were supposed to be . . . well, maybe not his children, exactly, but definitely the only kids in his life. We were a kind of family. We were supposed to be special. But this made me wonder. Did he have a group in Russia, too, and China? Was there an Australian version of me? And if so, did he wear bow ties with boomerangs on them?

Joaquim returned to the table. He tapped the picture. "Your friend—he knows Pepedro?"

"Who's Pepedro?" Ava asked.

"The boy," Joaquim answered. "Pepedro is the future of the Seleção, the future of Brazil."

I leaned toward Ava. "He's a soccer star," I explained. "The Seleção is another name for the national team."

"What's wrong with his foot?" she asked.

"Nothing!" Joaquim answered. "His left foot is brilliant. He can score from anywhere on the field with that foot. Once I saw him play at a small neighborhood field. He struck the ball so hard that he broke the window of a passing truck. The man who was driving was angry at first, but when he saw that it was Pepedro, he said he was honored and that he would never have the window repaired. Pepedro is more than a celebrity here. If I had to guess, I would say that his left foot alone is worth a million dollars."

"Seriously?" I asked.

"In Brazil, we do not joke about football."

Ava pointed to the printout. "Who's the girl?"

"His older sister, Alicia."

"Do you remember what they were talking about?" Matt asked. "Or maybe why they were meeting?"

Joaquim held his hands out wide. "No. That is their business. Mine is to feed them."

"Okay, so how do we find them?" I asked.

Joaquim grabbed the paper. "Your friend? I don't know. Pepedro and Alicia? This boy cannot walk down the street without dozens of people following him for an autograph, so they are very private." Joaquim stood and turned his head, looking back over his shoulder. A smile formed in the shade of his beard. "But Dona Maria might be able to help."

"Who is Dona Maria?" Ava asked.

The owner nodded toward the center of the room. "She is seated over there, with the mayor."

"Is she a politician or something?" Matt asked.

"No, a woman of business. She owns many companies and she knows every important person in Manaus. I will talk to her," he said. He reached across the table and slid the dish of pineapple sorbet in front of me. "And you will finish your dessert."

The sorbet was totally delicious, and while shoveling huge scoops into my mouth, I studied the old woman across the room. Her frizzy gray hair was tied up in a bun. Her eyebrows looked like they'd been drawn on with a black Sharpie. Her chin was long and slightly twisted, and I wanted her to have a wart on the end of it. No, three warts. But I couldn't see any warts.

We'd been waiting for at least ten minutes when Joaquim finally approached her table. He squatted next to her, respectfully. After whispering a few words and pointing our way, he showed her the printout. Dona Maria pulled a pair of eyeglasses from a shiny pocketbook and leaned forward as she studied the photo. Then she removed her eyeglasses, spoke briefly to Joaquim, and waved him away with a dismissive flick of her hand.

"That didn't look good," Ava said.

Joaquim zigzagged between the tables, passed Ava the

58

printout, and slapped a business card down on the white linen cloth. I grabbed it. "You're in luck," he said. "She says to go to her factory at nine o'clock tomorrow morning, and she will help you in any way that she can."

4

THE GRANDMOTHER OF THE IPHONE

THE NEXT MORNING, A BLACK LIMOUSINE PULLED TO A stop in front of the busted front steps of our small hotel. The rain was light, and the limo, despite a few dents, was stunningly beautiful. Matt swung his laptop bag over his shoulder—he'd just sewn a new NASA patch onto the flap—and hurried down the steps. We'd been planning to call a taxi, but this was way better. "Are you sure that's for us?" I asked.

The passenger side front window rolled down. The driver leaned over and waved us forward. He was wearing a bright orange polo shirt; I'd been hoping for one of those black chauffeur suits. Matt produced the business card and the man nodded.

"Dona Maria must have sent it," Matt said.

Ava elbowed me. "Stop smiling," she said. "This is serious."

Sure, I knew that. Hank was missing. We were in a foreign country. But we were getting into a limo. And I really,

really, really like limos. Inside, the leather seats were torn and cracked in places. The televisions didn't work. And I didn't care. I leaned back and stretched my legs. Matt jumped in shotgun and the driver stared at him for five solid seconds. No words were needed. My brother moved to the back and sat facing us as the limo cruised through Manaus, rolling through red lights and speeding through greens. At one point, we cut across a sidewalk to pass a smoke-spewing delivery truck.

The night before, we'd done a little research in our room and discovered that we'd be visiting a factory in an area of the city known as Zona Franca. That translates to Free Zone, but it doesn't mean you get free stuff there. Instead, it means the businesses there don't have to pay taxes. Although Manaus is officially known as the gateway to the Amazon, it's also the gadget capital of South America. All the smartphones and iPads and laptops in Brazil are assembled in Manaus, and we found out that Dona Maria didn't just own a few companies. Ava jumped around online and discovered at least a dozen. But one interested us more than the rest. Dona Maria was the first person to bring smartphones to South America, and she still made more of them at her factory in Manaus than anyone else on the continent.

In Brazil, she was known as the grandmother of the iPhone.

61

Ava yawned. After we'd done a little homework on Dona Maria, she'd borrowed Matt's laptop and worked past midnight. I didn't understand what she was doing, exactly, but it had something to do with Hank's satellite. Ava figured out that it had been flying over the rainforest every few days. That probably wasn't a coincidence. So she was hoping the CubeSat might give us some clue to Hank's location.

Unfortunately, she hadn't found any hints yet.

Dona Maria's factory was a squat cement building as wide as several football fields and surrounded by low rusted fences. The front gate was wide open, and we drove straight through. I was expecting armed guards. Maybe a helicopter circling overhead. Even a few robots with machine guns wouldn't have surprised me. But we cruised up to the main entrance without pausing and walked straight inside.

A long hallway stretched ahead of us. The light was yellow and dull. The air tasted like dust and metal. Machines whirred and hissed and beeped in the distance, and ice-cold air blasted out of a vent near the ceiling. In the center of the hall, Dona Maria balanced on a dark metal cane, waiting.

"You're late," she said. She smelled like cigar smoke, and her voice was younger than the rest of her, as if someone Min's age were trapped inside that wrinkled shell. "You're late," she repeated, "and I don't like to waste time."

She tapped her cane on the floor three times. Maybe it was the number of taps. Or all the wrinkles on her old face. I don't know why, exactly, but I pictured an earthquake spreading out from beneath the cane, a crack in the floor and the earth below swallowing me whole. She stared at the cane and sneered, then tapped it on the floor three times again, harder. A small green light in the handle began flashing. The old woman turned around and slid her left foot forward. Then she bent her knees so that she was squatting slightly. I couldn't tell if she was trying to let one go or getting ready for a race. None of us are athletic, exactly. But I was pretty certain we could all take a seventy-something-year-old grandma in a sprint. "Follow me," she said, "if you can keep up."

And then she bolted.

Yes, it was a foot race, but not a fair one, and certainly not the kind we'd expected. Dona Maria stayed in that staggered, crouched position and rocketed down the hall as if she'd been launched out of a giant slingshot. She slowed at the next corner, then grabbed a pole to her right, swung through a turn, and disappeared into a different hall.

My sister had built a motorized skateboard once. His name was Pedro, and you pretty much rode him the same way. Crouched down, feet staggered. But Pedro slammed me into a pile of garbage bags and my hair smelled like hot

dogs for a week. "Is she hiding a miniature Pedro under there?" I asked.

"Pedro was not that fast," Ava said. She was staring. "Motorized shoes, maybe?"

Matt stroked his chin. "Right, but she controls them with the cane. How?"

"Bluetooth?" Ava suggested.

"Uh, guys?" I said, pointing down the hall. "We're going to lose her. Maybe you could talk while we run?"

At the corner, there was no sign of Dona Maria, but a man in a white coat pointed to his left. Instead of stairs, a ramp sloped gently up to the second floor. I tripped. Below me, Matt laughed. Then he tripped, too.

Thank you, universe.

Ava hurried past us.

We were panting when we reached her office. Dona Maria was already standing behind an enormous wooden desk. She plugged one end of a power cable into an outlet behind her, the other end into her right boot. A thick, half-smoked cigar rested in a silver ashtray on the desk. Nearly a dozen business cards were neatly lined up along one edge. A two-foot-long, finely carved nameplate faced the door. I pointed. "Dona Maria Aparecida Oliveiros Dos Santos," I said, pronouncing each word slowly. "You Brazilians really do like your names."

"A name is history," she said. "So is this desk. It belonged to Dom Pedro II." The old woman moved her hands across the polished surface. "He was a large man. He sat. I stand."

The geniuses didn't respond. But I remembered that name from my reading. "He was the emperor, right?" I asked.

"Very good."

Confident, I rattled off a few facts I remembered from my reading, ending with one of the more surprising ones. "I believe he also introduced the chicken to Brazil."

"What? Why do you speak of chickens? This is not true," she said. She licked her lips like she was trying to get rid of a bad taste. "Now, show me your photograph."

As Ava pulled off her backpack to get the folded print-out, I motioned to the business cards, silently asking if I could help myself. Dona Maria nodded and I grabbed one of each. Embarrassed, Matt lifted his hand to his face. Once I was finished, I took out my notebook and scribbled a few details, including the woman's full name. I added a note about looking up the chicken thing, too. Where had I gotten that idea?

On the far side of her desk, there was a pile of tickets that read "Teatro Amazonas" on top. She slapped my hand as I turned one around to read the small print. "Those are for the opening night at the opera house," she said. "I have

66

a private booth. Many important people will be there. The mayor will be my guest. Maybe the chief of police. He is a friend, too. There will be famous footballers. Celebrities." She shrugged. "I know them all. They are all good friends."

"Can we come?" I asked.

She laughed hysterically, then lifted her fist to her mouth and began coughing. Matt leaned forward like he was going to help her, but she held up her hand, signaling him to wait. Then she pointed to her cigar. "Don't smoke, my friends," she said. "These will kill you."

My sister slid the printout across the desk and took my phone out of her pocket. Dona Maria glanced at the screen before eyeing the picture. "You should follow me on Twitter," she said. Without looking up, she pointed to her office door. Instead of her name, her Twitter handle was printed on the glass. "I have many followers. So," she said, turning the printout around in her hands, "are you looking for Dr. Witherspoon, too?"

The three of us glanced at one another. "You know him?" Ava asked.

"Of course I know him. I told you, I know every important person in Manaus. Even the visitors."

My sister leaned forward and rested her elbows on Dona Maria's desk. "Do you know why he'd be meeting with these kids?"

67

"He doesn't even like sports," I pointed out.

Dona Maria glared at Ava's elbows. My sister stood back. "I can think of a reason," the old woman said, sliding the printout back across the desk to Ava. "Pepedro is not only a soccer prodigy. He and his sister are the children of very skilled guides. They grew up touring the jungle with their parents. They know the rainforest as well as anyone."

"So you think their parents led Hank into the jungle?"

"No, the parents are dead for two years," she said. "I think maybe Pepedro and Alicia gave your friend some advice. Maybe they suggested some places to explore. Maybe they even led him themselves. Do you have any clues where in the rainforest he might be?"

"We have an idea," Ava said.

"An idea?" Dona Maria pressed.

Ava rocked her head back and forth. "I'm getting closer. I'll figure it out."

A faint beep sounded beneath the desk. "What was that?" I asked.

"My boots," Dona Maria said. "They are quick to charge, but quick to run out of energy, too." She laid one hand on the desk for balance, then reached down and switched the power cable from one boot to the other. "It is very, very frustrating. Now, back to your friend. . . . You think you will know soon, young lady?"

My sister started to reply, but I cut her off. "Maybe," I said. "But until then, we don't know much at all. That's why we need to find these kids."

"You have contacted him? Dr. Witherspoon?"

"Yes," Matt said, "but he hasn't responded to a single e-mail in weeks."

"Not even from his girlfriend," Ava added.

"She's not his girlfriend," Matt said. "He'd tell us."

Dona Maria was watching my sister. "So you cannot contact him, and you don't know where he is exactly, but you want to go look for him anyway."

"Precisely," I said.

"This is a crazy idea," she said. My sister muttered the beginnings of a reply, but Dona Maria waved her off. "No, no. I like crazy. I will help you."

"Do you think these kids would take us?" Matt asked.

"Can you help us find them?" Ava added.

Dona Maria nodded. "Yes, I can help you find them. Will they take you? That I don't know. I will text Alicia for you, but she will not answer right away."

"Why not?" Matt asked.

"Because Pepedro is playing today. A little pickup game in the center of the city." Dona Maria reached for her phone, tapped and swiped at the screen, then showed it to Ava. "Alicia tweeted about the game an hour ago."

"What's the address?" Matt asked. "We should go."

"You'll never get to talk to them there," Dona Maria said. "There will be too many people. But if you tell me the name of your hotel, I'll have her contact you there."

Normally, that plan would have been fine. But Matt was right when he'd bounced that sweaty sock ball off my head the day before. We hadn't flown to Brazil to sit in our hotel room. Waiting wasn't an option. "That would be great," I said, "but we're going to go, anyway. Just in case. Would you mind writing down the address of the field?"

The old woman shrugged and scribbled the names of the intersecting streets on a piece of notepaper, then handed it to Ava. "And your hotel?" she asked again. "In case you don't get to talk to them, I want to be able to reach you."

"The Hotel Magnificent," I said.

She winced as if she'd just had her finger pricked by a needle. "Not so magnificent."

My brother was already backtracking toward the door. "We should try to catch them before the game starts," he suggested.

Ava looked up from the notepaper. "How far away is this? Will we get there on time if we leave now?"

"Now? No. If you wanted to get there on time, you should have left ten minutes ago."

A long, heartfelt thank-you from each of us would have been appropriate. Maybe some gracious handshakes. Even a bow. Instead, the three of us shouted our thank-yous over our shoulders as we sprinted for the limo.

71

5

THE BOY WITH THE MILLION-DOLLAR FOOT

OBVIOUSLY I WASN'T AROUND WHEN THE BEATLES OR ELVIS were at their peak, and I was barely in preschool during the prime years of Bieber Fever, but I'd have to guess that the madness surrounding Pepedro was close to what those superstars experienced. As we drove across the city, Ava researched the young star. She discovered that he didn't actually play for a team yet. Instead, he'd show up at pickup games, or appear at the last minute and play in charity football matches with older players. Each time he did run onto the field, though, he mesmerized everyone with his footwork and the amazing power and accuracy of his left-footed shot. There were hundreds of clips of him on YouTube and countless photos and videos posted across social media. So we shouldn't have been surprised when we couldn't even get close to the outdoor field, which was surrounded on all sides by two-story-tall buildings and houses.

At least a dozen streets led straight to the edge of the grass, but the pavement was packed with people trying to get close enough to see the prodigy play. Fans were on roof-tops and leaning out of apartment windows. People leaned ladders against buildings and sat on the steps like they were bleachers. Someone was piloting a drone, too, and I swear there were nearly as many selfie sticks as there were people, only everyone was holding them up to film the play instead of themselves.

The car barely inched forward. The traffic and crowds were too dense. None of the people walking in front of us were moving out of the way. A woman in a black-and-red-striped soccer jersey turned and flicked her hair at our limo. The driver shouted something at her.

"Could we try another street? Another way in?" I suggested.

Ava translated for me.

The driver shrugged, held up his hands, and answered in Portuguese. "He says there's no point," Ava explained.

Two old dudes chewing on cigars scurried alongside our car, balancing on canes. Someone Matt's age was holding a toddler on his shoulders. A couple wearing matching soccer jerseys and matching fanny packs were pressing into the group, too. They looked like Americans. Crowds of teens were darting between people, kicking soccer balls along the dirt. Construction workers with dust-covered T-shirts stood on their toes, hoping for a better look. A boy and a girl who were probably close to my age cut in front of our car. The boy wore a thin hooded sweatshirt. His steps were short and uneven and he never lifted his eyes from the pavement. I propped myself higher in my seat for a better view. A tattered soccer ball rolled along at his feet. He tapped it forward, never too far from his toes. The girl at his side was grabbing his elbow, frowning as she looked for openings in the wall of people. She slapped the hood of the limo as our driver edged forward, squinting as she glared through the windshield. Her face was round, her hair dark as the night sky. She yanked the boy away from the car. He still didn't look up or lose the ball.

Our driver stopped and leaned toward the windshield. He squinted, staring back at the girl, then grabbed his phone and called someone. He whispered, then waited. The two kids turned left, away from the crowds, and our driver followed them.

"Why are we going this way?" Ava asked. She repeated the question in Portuguese.

The driver ignored her.

Ava leaned out the window, eyeing the tops of the buildings. "What if we get up on the roof? If I had Betsy with me it would be easy."

"Should we just get out and walk?" Matt suggested.

I watched the two kids.

74

"We're here to talk to Pepedro, not watch him play," Ava answered. "He's probably out there already. I think we're better off waiting and trying to catch him on his way out."

The limo rolled to a stop. The girl with the night-black hair glared back at our driver. Then she and her companion turned again, backtracking and walking alongside our car in the opposite direction, toward the river of soccer fans rushing to the field. I reached around Ava and opened the door. The girl nearly banged into it, then walked around and peered inside at us. The boy was still at her side. His hoodie was old and worn, but his soccer cleats looked new. The bulge in his socks suggested he was wearing shin guards, too. He rested his foot atop the scuffed soccer ball.

His left foot.

"Want a ride?" I asked.

The boy glanced up at the girl. Clearly she made their decisions. My brother grabbed my sleeve. "Jack, what are you . . ." He stopped and stared at the kids and the ball. "Wait, is that Pepedro?" he asked in a whisper.

I took a second to savor my minor accomplishment. I was a step ahead of Matt. Maybe a half step ahead of Ava, too. And I deserved to enjoy that feeling. Like the last bite of that pineapple sorbet, I wanted to let it linger. But the girl started to close the limo door and move on. "Yes, Matt," I said. "That's Pepedro, and this is his sister, Alicia. Am I

75

right? Ava, could you translate? Ask them to come inside for a few minutes. Tell them we have a few questions."

Alicia wagged her finger. "I understand English," she said. "But I do not understand why you are asking us to get into your limousine."

Two burly men in green-and-yellow soccer jerseys pushed past the kids. "Two reasons," I said. "First, it's quiet in here, out of the crowds."

"And what is the other reason?"

"We're friends of Henry Witherspoon," Matt said.

The girl's head jerked back slightly.

A woman with wide hips and swinging elbows nearly knocked over Pepedro. A group of men marched past, chanting and singing. More and more people were pressing closer to the field. Music was blaring. A bottle of beer shattered on the pavement behind the kids. Still, the girl tried to close the door again.

Then the woman who'd hip-checked Pepedro spun around. She held her hands to her face and pointed at the boy with the million dollar foot. An older man beside her then recognized the young soccer star and shuffled toward him with a Sharpie and a half-crumpled piece of paper. The woman grabbed the marker, untucked her T-shirt, and held it out for Pepedro to sign. The madness spread like lice.

Suddenly everyone was shoving their way to the limo, holding out smartphones, begging for selfies.

Alicia pulled the door open wider and pretty much threw her brother into the limo as our driver reversed out of the crowd. He was leaning back and looking through the rear window. Honestly, the guy might have been better at driving backward.

The boy with the million dollar foot exhaled as he and his sister settled into the cracked leather seats. Matt switched sides and sat between Ava and me, and the girl spoke to the driver in Portuguese.

"You're telling him to get out of here?" Ava asked.

"Won't his team be disappointed?" I added.

The girl sighed as she stared through the window at the growing crowds. "This is just pickup. My brother is not letting down his teammates. Maybe the crowd, but it's okay, because this is not safe for my brother. This is like São Paulo. Maybe worse."

On the plane I'd read a little about São Paulo, a sprawling city of twenty million people. "What happened in São Paulo?" I asked.

"It was madness," Pepedro said. "The crowds grew so fast that they began to press in on the pitch."

"The field," Matt said. "In America we call it the field."

"You're not in America," Alicia reminded him. "You are in Brazil."

I laughed. Pepedro did, too. Then his smile vanished as he recalled the event. "We had to crawl out, like animals through the brush. Like peccaries. Pigs."

"That sounds terrible."

Alicia shrugged. "Yes, but we survived. I'm Alicia. This is Pepedro. But you know that. You are Hank's family?" she asked.

I waited for Matt to answer. Or Ava. But neither of them said anything. "Well," I began, "I mean . . . I guess you could say . . ."

"Sort of?" Matt offered.

Ava inched forward to the edge of the seat. "Did Hank say we were his family?"

"Maybe I misunderstood," Alicia said. "He showed us some pictures of you." She pointed to me. "Where is the funny little tie?"

"My bow tie? I—"

"Why are you here?" Alicia asked. "Did you come to watch my brother play?"

"No," Ava said.

Someday, I hope to teach my sister that brutal honesty isn't always the best strategy. "Well, yes, we did," I said. "Ava's just joking. We love soccer. Really. And we've heard such amazing things about your left foot, Pepedro. But we do have a few other questions for you."

Alicia crossed one leg over the other and raised her eyebrows. "Yes?"

Ava didn't hesitate. "Did Hank hire you as guides?"

"Yes," Pepedro replied.

"Where did he want you to take him?"

"The rainforest."

"No," Ava said. "Where in the rainforest? And why?"

Matt leaned forward. "What was he looking for?"

"Why don't you ask him yourself?"

"We haven't heard from him for three weeks," I explained. "We're worried he might be in danger."

"Yes," Alicia replied. "He might be."

Ava leaned forward. "We need to know everything."

The limo was finally clear of the crowd, and our driver was talking quietly on his phone. Alicia spoke to him over her shoulder as her brother removed his shin guards and unlaced his cleats, switching them for a pair of scuffed canvas sneakers. The driver snapped his phone into a dashboard mount and steered onto a quieter street.

Alicia gazed out the window at the passing buildings. "Do you know what I do? My brother, he kicks a ball. He kicks so well that people have already offered to pay us millions of dollars if he will kick the ball for their team when he is older."

"But you're only like twelve years old," Ava said.

"Thirteen," Pepedro said. "But this doesn't matter. If you can kick, they will pay you now, so you don't play for someone else later."

Alicia removed her backpack, pulled out a green bandage, reached down, and waved to him to lift up his foot. He turned and swung his leg onto the seat between them, and she started wrapping his left foot in the bandage, right over his sneaker. "Me," Alicia began, "I think this is silly. Millions of dollars, all for *o jogo bonito*, the beautiful game? Ridiculous. Pepedro, he thinks it is silly, too."

The blank expression on his face suggested he didn't completely agree.

"Totally ridiculous," Ava said.

"Absurd," Matt added. "Talented young scientists can barely pay their rent."

"Well," I said, "I think it's awesome that people want to pay you millions of dollars to kick a ball."

Now Pepedro smiled. Alicia nodded. "Yes, maybe. And we should let them. Absolutely! But . . ." She held up her index finger like a scolding teacher. It seemed really long. Was it? Or was it an illusion? If I could have frozen time, I would've stopped to measure it. "But," she repeated, "we must be certain that he is not taken advantage of by these teams and businesses. This is my role. I review the deals, and we have not yet found a deal that is good for my brother."

"Alicia is my agent," Pepedro said.

She finished wrapping his foot, then patted it gently and leaned back in her seat. "This is why we protect him and his foot. This foot is worth millions of American dollars. Maybe more. These teams who want him . . . they will pay us money now, but then we will be tied to them forever. Pepedro will not be able to make his own choices. We don't just want money. We want freedom. So we wait."

The limo was accelerating. Our driver was glancing in the rearview mirror. Alicia opened the miniature fridge and removed several ice-cold cans of soda. Why hadn't I thought to look in there? The cans were red and green and yellow. She called up to the driver, then passed one to each of us after he responded. "Guarana," she explained. "Brazilian soda. Very delicious."

Matt popped the top and sipped. "It's like ginger ale," he said.

"No," Alicia said. "It's like Guarana."

My sister was holding her cold,

unopened can in both hands. "You were talking about money and freedom," she said. "What does that have to do with Hank?"

"Everything."

"Everything?"

"No, maybe not everything. Sometimes, this choice to not accept a contract is a little painful. Sometimes, we need money. So when your friend Hank asked if he could hire us to take him into the jungle, we accepted."

"Aren't there other guides?" Ava asked.

"There are many other guides," Pepedro replied. "But they don't know what we know."

"And what do you two know that's so special?"

82

"We know how to find the giant eels."

6

ODORASED

THE LIMO ROLLED THROUGH QUIET, TREE-LINED STREETS as Alicia and her brother told us their story. Their parents were expert rainforest guides, and several years earlier they had made an important discovery, a species that was much larger and more powerful than any of the known electric eels. Naturally, my brother knew the Latin name, *Electrophorus electricus magnus*. And he knew the name of the scientist credited with its discovery, too.

"Our parents led this scientist into the rainforest to study the eels," Pepedro explained.

"He barely mentioned them in his research paper," Alicia added.

"That's not fair," Ava said.

"Yes, well, our parents didn't care," Alicia said. "Some years passed, and then your friend Hank read the scientist's paper on the eels. He wanted to come to Brazil to study the creatures himself, so the scientist sent him to our parents. There was just one problem."

"They were dead?"

"Jack!"

"Sorry, Dona Maria told us—"

"No, it's okay. You're right. They were dead. Our mother was killed by a poisonous frog and my father was eaten by piranhas."

The three of us fell silent. My mouth might have hung open. A few seconds passed. Alicia had this weird, strained look on her face, like she was holding back gas. "Wait, are you serious?" I asked.

She laughed. "No! Car accident."

"I'm sorry," Pepedro said. "My sister thinks she is funny."

"I am funny," she insisted. She appealed to Ava. "That was funny, right?"

My sister winced.

"A little dark," Matt said.

"But frogs always make a story funnier," I added. "Frogs and goats."

Now it was the Brazilians who were silent. Sometimes I wished there was a guard between my brain and my mouth. A little guy who listened to my ideas and decided whether my mouth should voice them. He'd be pretty busy, constantly grabbing thoughts and tossing them back down into my mind's garbage bin. He'd probably have a long beard, too. Maybe he'd wear overalls. And when he wasn't working, he'd play the harmonica.

"Okay," Matt resumed, "so Hank finds you instead, and he asks you to help him find these eels?"

"He wrote an e-mail to our parents," Alicia explained. "We still have the address for their guide business. So we told him to meet us at a restaurant here in Manaus—"

"Saudade," I said.

"Yes, that's right. How did you know that?"

I wanted to tell them about the matchbook and how the geniuses didn't know why Hank kept it in the bathroom. Instead, I pointed to Ava. "She figured it out. Anyway, you met him, and then what?"

"He was surprised to meet young people," Alicia said. "But he mentioned something about knowing a few talented children himself." My brother blushed. "He agreed to pay us to help him find the eels. We departed a few days later and journeyed down the river. We found some beautiful eels. Very big. Huge electric fields. Your friend Hank was using all kinds of instruments to study them. Everything was going very well."

"Until?"

"Until we learned that we were not alone," Alicia added.

"A small group of scouts for a logging company was hiking through the same section of the jungle, marking trees that they wanted to cut down."

85

"That's illegal, right?" Matt asked. "You can't just cut down trees in the rainforest."

"Yes," Pepedro said. "Unfortunately, it is also a very easy law to break. The loggers can destroy entire sections of the jungle before anyone notices."

The driver swung the limo off the quiet side street and onto a crowded avenue. Alicia leaned toward the window to study the street signs. She squinted, then sat up. "Your friend Hank was furious. He was yelling at them about carbon sinks. And they had guns!"

Leave it to Hank to lecture a group of armed men about climate change. "Yep, that's Hank," I said.

"By the way, what are these carbon sinks?" Pepedro asked.

Quickly, Ava explained: "Too much carbon in the atmosphere traps heat, which causes the planet to warm."

"Climate change," Pepedro said.

"Exactly," Ava answered. "The trees in the Amazon rainforest basically suck carbon out of the air and trap it. So they help fight warming."

"And since the rainforest stores all that carbon," Matt added, "that means if you cut down the trees, bacteria and other microscopic forms of life attack the wood and release the carbon dioxide into the air."

"Back to the loggers," I said. "Did they kidnap him?"

Alicia sipped her soda before responding. "Kidnap? No, no, no. They let us go and warned that they would shoot us if we ever returned."

"He went back, though, didn't he?" Matt asked.

"Yes," Alicia answered. "He had some kind of plan to use satellites to save the rainforest."

Instantly I imagined a fleet of tiny satellites drifting overhead, tracking the illegal loggers, then blasting their chainsaws with space lasers. The beams would be blue. Or maybe green. Because they'd belong to the good guys. But would that even work? Did satellites have lasers? Luckily, the little harmonica player stopped me from suggesting the possibility.

"How many times did he go back?" Ava asked.

"This last time was the fourth," Alicia replied. "We didn't go back with him, though. He didn't want to put us in danger, so he insisted on going himself. Each time he came down to Brazil, he'd treat us to a nice dinner. That man loved steak."

"Loves," Ava corrected her. "Plus he's a vegetarian."

"Not anymore," Pepedro said.

My sister frowned. They were acting like they knew him better than we did. She didn't like that. And neither did I.

For a minute, we were all silent. The pieces of this puzzle just weren't fitting together. I finished my drink, then tilted

87

my head back and tipped the can upside down, hoping for a few more drops. When I was finished, I caught Pepedro smiling at me. These Brazilians were really proud of their soda.

Outside, the traffic was only getting worse. A light mist was falling, making it difficult to see. Alicia kept rolling down her window quickly, trying to spot the street signs. She spoke with the driver in Portuguese before explaining that she didn't know the route he'd chosen.

Matt breathed in deep. "You have to take us."

"Where?" Alicia asked.

"To the jungle! We need to find Hank."

Alicia sat back and smiled. "This is good."

"So you'll take us?" Ava asked.

"Maybe. First, we must negotiate. I need some practice before we decide to choose a team for my brother in a few years. So," she said, crossing her arms as she leaned back in her seat, "how much can you pay?"

"Whatever it takes," Ava answered.

"Well, not exactly," Matt said.

"Alicia," Pepedro started, "I don't think this is the time to practice——"

"How much?" Ava asked.

Quietly, Alicia quoted a number. "That's reais, the Brazilian currency," she said.

Ava closed her eyes, converting the figure into dollars. She muttered the number under her breath. "That's a lot, but we can do it," she said.

Alicia frowned. "I should've started higher."

"No, that's plenty high," Matt said. "That's way too much."

"Matt, this is Hank we're talking about."

Ava was right. What was his problem? "The flights were one thing, Matt," I added. "The hotel, too. But we shouldn't be worrying about money now. This is too important."

"Our price stays," Alicia insisted.

My brother was staring at the floor. "We can't hire them," he mumbled.

Why was he being so stubborn? "We have to," I replied.

"We can't hire them, okay? We don't have any money."

"There's probably an ATM somewhere—"

"No," Matt said. "You don't get it . . ."

"This really isn't the right time to be cheap," Ava said.

Matt laughed uncomfortably. "I agree! Totally. But here's the thing . . . see, we're kind of . . ." As his voice faded, he started wringing his hands together in front of his chest.

"We're kind of what?" I asked. "What are you talking about?"

Finally my brother blurted out the truth. "We're kind of out of money." He exhaled. He smiled. Then he stuck out

89

his tongue and breathed out again. "Phew. Wow! That feels good. Amazing, really. You have no idea how long I've been holding that in."

Turning to face him, Ava asked, "Matt, what are you talking about?"

My brother shrugged. "We have twenty bucks in the bank. At most. Maybe less, if Jack forgot to cancel his subscription to the Swank Club."

"The what?" Alicia asked.

"Nothing," I replied.

And it really was nothing, considering that my monthly membership to the Swank Club meant I got either a new bow tie or a new pair of colorful socks in the mail each month. Even if I had canceled my membership, twenty bucks wasn't going to get us a guide. That wouldn't be enough money to hire someone to walk us down the street, let alone through the jungle.

The limo accelerated, then stopped as the cars ahead of us braked. I pushed out with my feet to prevent myself from landing in Pepedro's lap. That would've been awkward. And I kind of wished our driver was going backward again.

"Credit cards?" Ava asked.

"Maxed out. We can't put another dollar on them."

"Wait," Ava said. "Reboot. How did this happen?"

Matt explained everything. Basically, we make all our money from the sales of our book of poems, *The Lonely*

Orphans. I talked Hank into giving us a small allowance for helping out around the lab—you're welcome, siblings—and a few dollars dribbled in now and then from the ads that ran with my YouTube video. But most of our cash came from book sales, and according to Matt, those sales had been plummeting. Not only that, but our expenses kept rising. The rent for our apartment had increased. Ava always needed new equipment for her projects. Matt had bought himself a new telescope and a high-powered laptop that quickly became his favorite thing in the world. And one of us had a taste for rare and expensive basketball sneakers. Was five hundred dollars too much to pay for a pair of high-tops worn in an actual NBA game? No. Of course not.

Anyway, Matt detailed how money was flooding out of our bank account but only trickling in. He'd been trying to make it all work. He even wrote a sequel to *The Lonely Orphans*, but the new book was rejected by thirty different publishers. Apparently people were tired of orphan verses. The latest thing, Matt said, was cat poetry.

Alicia interrupted before he could continue. "These poems are written by cats?" she asked.

"What? No. How would a cat write a poem?"

"With its paws?" I suggested. "Maybe it could have a special pen."

"The point is, we can't even pay our rent next month."

He stared across at Alicia and Pepedro. "So we definitely can't hire a guide. You two are our only hope."

"It's impossible. We'd never find him. The rainforest is enormous."

"But if we look for the eels, we could find Hank," I noted.

"These eels are spread across thousands of square kilometers, an area bigger than some of your American states. Even if we did help you, we could never find him."

Staring out the window, Alicia held up her finger again and turned toward the front. "Sorry. One minute. I need to talk to our driver. I don't understand where we are going."

The car slowed and turned. My sister was squinting now. She leaned toward the window and studied the street signs at the nearest corner. Alicia questioned the driver in Portuguese and shrugged when he answered. "You said someone sent you this limo?" she asked. "Who?

"Dona Maria," I answered.

"Are you sure?"

No. Not really. My siblings didn't look too convinced, either. "I'm not positive, but I—"

"Wait," Ava said. She lowered her voice. "It couldn't have been Dona Maria. She didn't even know where we were staying until this morning. Remember? She made us write down our address when we left."

"So then who hired this limo?"

"I'll ask him," Pepedro offered. He called out to the driver in Portuguese.

The partition rose up from behind the Brazilians' seat. The glass sealed shut. The doors locked. The car turned out of the traffic and accelerated as the rain fell faster.

Alicia banged on the barrier. Matt leaned across and joined her. But our driver didn't even react. Ava yanked at the door handle. The windows wouldn't budge, either.

"What's going on?" I asked. "What's he doing?"

Pepedro was perfectly relaxed, as if we were sitting at lunch, talking about sandwiches, when he replied, "I believe we are being kidnapped."

Reaching forward, I pulled Matt away from the glass. He was going to break his hand. Over his shoulder, I glanced at the phone on the dashboard. The screen was bright green. A white telephone icon was visible in the lower right corner. The minutes and seconds were ticking onward. I pointed. "His phone's on speaker. Someone's been listening this whole time."

"Who?" Ava asked.

None of us knew. And none of us could figure out how to get out of that limousine. My sister started sorting through her backpack, searching for something that might help. Matt did the same, rooting through his canvas

93

laptop bag. But writing a new computer program or typing an e-mail wasn't going to save us now. In a rush, I dug through the contents of my own backpack. I had a few books about Brazil, my notebook, a granola bar, some extra cheese breads wrapped in a greasy napkin, and the Odoraser. I turned the device over in my hands. At that point, I'd used it ten or twelve times already and still hadn't let out the contents. Thousands or even millions of airplane hair spray particles and my own personal farticles were trapped inside.

The best inventions, as I once learned from Hank, sometimes have unexpected uses. The automobile, for example, was originally dreamed up as a way to wash underpants. Only later did engineers realize it might be a good way to move people around. Okay, so that might not be true. I forget the actual example Hank gave me. And anyway, the point is that I'd never thought of the Odoraser as a self-defense weapon. But we were desperate.

Behind the boy with the million dollar foot, there was a small opening in the glass partition about the size of a bank card, and a plastic door you could slide back and forth to pass money through to the driver. Squeezing between Pepedro and Alicia, I placed the device through the plastic gap and into the driver's section of the limo, then pressed the release button.

The Odoraser ejected its foul contents. The stench flowed throughout the front of the car. Only a few seconds passed before my farticles flooded the driver's nostrils. He coughed. He gagged. He lurched forward like he was ready to vomit. The limo swerved. I dropped the Odoraser onto his seat as he jammed on the brakes. The driver tried the door handle, but he'd locked himself in, too. Frantically pushing buttons, he unlocked the door and struggled out into the street, breathing deeply as the rain fell all around him.

I tried the back door opposite the driver's side. It opened. In his odor-crushed insanity, he'd unlocked everything. Alicia rushed out first. The rest of us tumbled to the curb behind her. Hands on his knees, still gathering air, the driver yelled at us in Portuguese.

My Odoraser was still in the front seat. I started to go get it, but Matt yanked on my arm. "Leave it, Jack!"

"Run!" Alicia said. "Run!"

A small, dark hole opened in my heart as I thought of my precious fart catcher lying alone on the front seat, abandoned after it had pretty much saved our lives. But I ran. The five of us tore past two restaurants and a juice bar. The rain was rushing down now. It felt like we were being pelted with hundreds of miniature water balloons. And we could run only so fast. The cracks and potholes turned the sidewalk into an obstacle course. Alicia was leading us, followed by Ava and Matt. Pepedro was right next to me, unwrapping his foot as we ran.

Then he stopped.

"Hurry!" I called back. "He's catching us!"

The driver was ten or fifteen parked cars away from us. Pepedro turned to face him. The driver slowed his pace, wiping the rain off his brow. His orange polo shirt was already soaked through. Alicia was calling to her brother. Matt and Ava were yelling. But Pepedro was not moving. His left foot was turning over a chunk of pavement the size and shape of a baseball. His head was tilted to one side. The rain was pelting him, pelting everything, but he didn't notice. The driver was slowly walking forward. His steps were heavy and menacing. I wanted to turn and run. Desperately. But even more than that, I wanted to see what Pepedro was going to do next.

The driver started to charge, splashing with each heavy step, and then Pepedro leaned forward, flicked the stone into the air with his left foot, waited until it dropped to the level of his knee, and struck. His leg moved like lightning, and the stone flew through the air, arcing over the parked cars before curving back to the right and striking the driver directly in the side of the head.

Instantly the man dropped to his knees, twisted, and

fell forward into a puddle. The boy with the million dollar foot put his hand on my shoulder. "We will do it for free," Pepedro said. "We will take you to the rainforest and find your friend Hank."

7

THE *VON HUMBOLDT*

THE NEXT MORNING WE TRUDGED THROUGH LIGHT BUT steady rain to the Port of Manaus. Towering cruise ships were docked in the distance. Tall cranes picked up enormous, rusted containers and stacked them on the decks of boats that looked like fallen, floating apartment buildings. Each of us was carrying an overstuffed backpack filled with camping equipment, including rain gear and hammocks and ropes and all kinds of dehydrated food and plastic bowls and cutlery. My sister also insisted on bringing Betsy, and Matt found a way to cram his laptop into his bag. I didn't bother asking why he needed a computer in the jungle.

The walk was painful because we'd barely slept. After we'd almost been kidnapped, we decided it wouldn't be safe to stay in our hotel. So we grabbed our bags and spent the night with Alicia and Pepedro, who lived in a single-room house in a wildly crowded neighborhood called a "favela." Their chairs were plastic milk crates. Their window curtains were old soccer jerseys. And forget beds. The place had only two small cots. Pepedro insisted on giving his to Ava, but she refused. So I took his bed instead, and I still had one of the worst nights of sleep of my life. I should've just hit the rug like the others.

The good news? Not only did we have guides, we'd also secured a ride down the river. As promised, Dona Maria had texted Alicia—several times, in fact—and our new friend finally called the grandmother of the iPhone and told her all about our situation. The old woman felt terrible and asked how she could help. Alicia explained that we needed a boat to take us deep into the jungle, and within thirty minutes, Dona Maria had everything arranged.

Now Alicia was leading us beneath the cranes toward the bow of one of the huge ships. Squeezed between that tanker and another, a long and narrow boat was tied to the dock. Next to the floating buildings, it looked like it had been shot with a shrink ray. But it was beautiful. The bow and stern were open, lined with polished wooden benches, and a large cabin rose up in the center, its roof scattered with instruments. We stopped a city block away.

"That's our boat," Alicia said. "The *Von Humboldt*."

"It looks brand-new," Matt remarked.

"Where's the captain?" Ava asked.

We walked closer. I called out, "Ahoy, there!"

Ava glared at me. "Seriously, Jack?"

What? I've always wanted to yell that.

A man hurried out of the cabin. He was Matt's height and dressed in running clothes and purple lacrosse shorts. His shoulders were wider than average, his jaw was thick and covered with a slight beard, and his hair was short on the sides and greasy on top. "Greetings! Welcome!"

Matt glanced at me. Dona Maria hadn't told us the captain was a foreigner. I'd just figured he'd be Brazilian. He didn't sound American, though. Or English.

"You're Bobby?" Alicia asked.

"I am! Captain Bobby. But you can just call me Captain, lass."

"Your accent," Ava said. "Is that Irish? Or Scottish?"

"Bit o' both! Welcome aboard the *Von Humbert*."

"You mean *Von Humboldt*, right?"

"Yes, that's what I said. Now come on, let's go. Throw your gear downstairs. The front cabin's mine. You can take the back ones."

"Don't you mean aft?" Matt asked.

"Aft?"

"Yes, you know—nautical terms. Forward instead of front. Aft instead of back. Below instead of downstairs. Starboard, port. Head for the bathroom."

Captain Bobby eyed Matt for a moment, then ignored

his comment completely. "Right, so we'll be leaving in five minutes. No point waiting around. Dona Maria didn't tell me where you want to go, though."

"East," Ava replied.

"Okay," Bobby said. "East is easy. Why don't you get settled in your cabins."

We climbed a narrow, steep ladder into a cramped galley. The boat's one head was next to the galley's sink. Our cabins in the stern were small enough for Smurfs, and there were only four tight bunks for the five of us. Matt bumped his head on a beam, and when he managed to twist himself into one of the bunks, he couldn't straighten out his legs. "I'll sleep on deck," he announced.

The engines began rumbling while we were still below. The boat lurched in reverse first, then stopped. I tripped and fell into my brother, then covered my nose. His pits needed an Odoraser implant.

"What?" he said. "I used deodorant."

"Use more."

The boat jumped forward before stopping again.

"What's he doing?" Pepedro asked.

We hurried up onto the deck. Ava pushed past me and leaped over the side. Was she bailing already?

"Ava, don't leave," Matt called out.

She was crouching next to one of the huge metal cleats

on the cement pier. "I'm not leaving," she said. She held up a thick rope. "I'm untying us."

Standing at the helm, our captain slid open a window and leaned out. "Good work! I was testing you, and you passed."

Normally a compliment like that would've forced a smile, but Ava's face was blank. She untied another line and climbed back aboard as the *Von Humboldt* steered away from the dock. Matt stood with Captain Bobby on the bridge, in front of the copilot's chair, watching through the windshield. Behind Matt, there was a long table with a cushioned bench that wrapped around three sides. A couch that could easily double as a bed stretched out behind the captain, and the stern was open. A few chairs and benches were lined up along the sides, and a large plastic case bolted to the deck held an inflatable emergency life raft. The "Do Not Open" sign was insanely tempting, but I resisted and unlatched another plastic case about the size of a miniature fridge. Inside, three gleaming machetes were clipped into place. I started to reach for one, but my sister told me to leave it alone. "We just got aboard, Jack," she said. "Can we avoid a stab wound?"

I grumbled and snapped the case shut.

The skies were blue and clear, so the Brazilians joined us at the stern, enjoying the air before the rains resumed.

Bobby was blasting music and shaking his hips as he stood at the helm.

"Where did Dona Maria find this guy?" Ava asked.

"Quiet—he's right there," I reminded her.

"He can't hear us," Ava replied.

"He's a little odd, but Dona Maria promised that he would take us where we needed to go," Alicia said. "That reminds me. Do we know any more about where Hank might be?"

"We do," Ava said.

The day before, as we hid out in the Brazilians' small home, Ava and Matt had spent a few more hours on the computer. Now my sister finally explained what they'd been doing. After they figured out that Hank's satellite was flying over the rainforest, they searched through a bunch of Hank's websites and found a page that featured a map. Not just any map, either, but one of the same region he'd visited with Pepedro and Alicia.

"Can we see it?" Alicia asked.

Ava hurried below and retrieved the laptop. Matt hated when we borrowed his gear without asking, but he was too busy trying to act like a riverboat captain to notice. Back in her seat, Ava opened the screen, then made me move to one side and Pepedro to the other, to protect the computer from river spray.

"I'm not online now, but we saved the page," Ava said, opening the file. The image was mostly the green tops of trees, with a few thin rivers winding through. But a number of small red circles were also scattered throughout the area. "See these dots?" she asked. "When we clicked through them, a list of dates popped up. Some of the dots had five or ten date stamps. Some had less. And when we clicked through a date, a close-up photo of that spot appeared."

"What's special about those locations?" Pepedro asked.

"I don't know," Ava admitted. "But this dot right here," she said, pointing to a spot in the upper right corner of the screen, "is the newest. There's just one date, and it was two days ago."

"So Hank was there two days ago?"

My sister shrugged. "Maybe? I don't know. But the oldest date in the list was a little less than three weeks ago."

"The last time we heard from Hank," I said.

"Right," Ava said.

"So maybe the satellite is tracking him somehow?" Alicia suggested.

My sister shrugged. "Maybe. All I know is that if we're going to start anywhere," she said, pointing to the dot in the upper right of the screen, "this makes the most sense."

Before any of us could reply, our captain yelled back at us with a smile. "What are you four doing back there?"

Ava closed the laptop. Matt caught her, and she hurried below without looking at him. I leaned over to Pepedro. "That spot Ava showed us," I began. "Do you know how to get there?"

Alicia patted me on the back. "Of course," she said.

The weather was kind enough to grant us a few rain-free hours. I thought we were on the Amazon itself, but the great waterway didn't really start until two other, smaller rivers merged. We were probably a half hour into the journey when Pepedro leaned to the right—or starboard, I guess— and pointed ahead. "You get to see one of the wonders of Manaus, the meeting of the waters."

The water beneath us was dark, almost black. But on the southern side, the water was a muddy, sandy color, kind of like one of the milky, sugary coffees from the plane. In the middle, the color switched from this dark black to milky brown, as if there were a thin, invisible wall stretching through the center of the river.

"How is that even possible?" I asked.

Alicia was biting her lip. "So beautiful. It's like magic, right?"

"It's not magic, it's science," Ava replied.

Then she started to explain how it worked. My brother caught us staring. He couldn't miss a chance to show off his knowledge, either, so he joined us at the stern and added in a few details. Apparently we were cruising through an area in which two smaller rivers flowed into one another to form the Amazon. At first, though, they mixed about as well as oil and water, because the northern one is much colder and denser. It gets its dark hue from all the plants that fall into the river upstream and dissolve. "Plus it runs much faster than the southern river, the Solimões," Matt added.

"And despite the dark color," Ava added, "it's one of the cleanest rivers in the world."

"Truly amazing," Captain Bobby said. "I didn't know that."

Mesmerized, we all gazed at the water.

Then I realized something.

Our captain was standing beside us.

At the stern.

I glanced toward the bridge. No one was at the helm. "Captain!" I yelled. "Who's driving?"

"Relax," Bobby laughed. "We're fine! The boat drives itself. Come on, I'll show you." He led us to the bridge and pointed at a map of the surrounding area on a high-definition touch screen. "All I have to do is pick our first stop tonight. Then she takes us there."

"How does it avoid obstacles?" Ava asked.

Captain Bobby shrugged. "I don't know."

Ava leaned out over the side and tried to study the

equipment and antennae on the roof. "What kind of sensors does it use?"

Captain Bobby held up his hands.

"What kind of algorithms is it running?" Matt added.

"Beats me," he replied. "I just drive her."

"Only you don't drive her," I noted.

He pointed at me. "Exactly!"

The geniuses were suddenly quiet, their brains tangled into knots. And I didn't know how to respond. As we cruised east down the river, Manaus became a memory. The two rivers finally blended into a milky brown. Thick, green jungle replaced the buildings on the shore, and the rain began again, forcing us into the cover of the cabin.

Every so often I'd spot a caiman swimming low in the brown water. Matt pointed out a few river otters, too. They were as large as me, gray and whiskered and slimy, as if they were covered in some kind of goo. A few smaller ones snaked around one another as we passed, slithering up the bank of the river into a narrow, dark hole below the exposed roots of a huge tree. I shivered as I watched. The otters were definitely going to turn up in my dreams.

"Fascinating," Matt said.

"No," I replied. "Creepy."

Rain began to fall again, and the five of us sat around the table as the boat steered itself east. Our captain stretched out on the long bench behind the pilot's seat and pulled a cap over his eyes. I figured he was going to take a nap. Instead, he asked, "So where am I taking you kids, exactly?"

"The rainforest," I said.

"Yeah, I know that," he said. "But where in the rainforest? It's a big place."

"Tomorrow we'll turn north up the Rio Jatapu," Alicia said.

Our captain yawned and said that would be fine.

That night, we anchored the boat in a deep pool on the banks of the river, and Bobby cooked us a huge pot of rice, beans, and some kind of bitter greens for dinner. The rain stopped once we finished eating. Moonlight shone between the clouds. Red dots glowed near the edge of the river. At first I thought the lights might be one of my siblings playing around with the laser pointers. But then I remembered my reading. The eyes of the caiman, the South American version of the crocodile, glowed an eerie red at night.

My row-mate on the plane had warned me about the noise. I figured the river would be quiet, though. Instead, the sounds of the jungle carried over the water. Birds were yelling at one another. Insects were buzzing wildly. Occasionally, something would holler or roar. I tried to spot the source of one of these sounds. But behind the caimans, all I could see were tall trees and dark shadows. I'm not a believer in Bigfoot. Hank and my siblings wouldn't let me latch on to a myth like that. Not even a really awesome one. But down in Brazil, some of the locals believe in a creature called the "Mapinguay," a sloth the size of an NFL lineman that stalks the jungle. The beast is basically the Amazonian version of Bigfoot. And as I stared into that thick, dark jungle, I wouldn't have been surprised if he'd popped his head out and waved.

8
HOOKING A MONSTER

THE NEXT MORNING, I ROLLED OVER IN MY CRAMPED COT and looked for my alarm clock. Then I remembered that we weren't home in our small apartment. We were on the Amazon River, Hank was missing, and our captain didn't know the difference between the bow and the stern. I tried to go back to sleep. I failed.

On deck, my siblings and Alicia were sitting at the table, eating. Pepedro was juggling in the back of the boat, and Bobby was dangling his legs over the bow, staring at the river as the boat cruised east.

"What's for breakfast?" I asked.

Ava leaned her bowl toward me, revealing more rice, beans, and greens. "Leftovers," she said.

"And he doesn't make breakfast sandwiches," Matt added. "So don't bother asking."

At lunch, Bobby served rice and beans again. I forced down a bowl, but I wasn't sure I could eat the same meal one more time. Pepedro, Alicia, and the geniuses weren't happy about our food, either, so we all decided to confront our captain.

"I thought you were going to bring your own food," Bobby admitted. "All I've got onboard is rice and beans."

"We brought food to take on our hike, but we need to save that," Alicia noted.

Off the port side of the boat, something splashed. Bobby pointed. "Hey, what if we drop anchor and catch some fish?"

"Have you ever fished this river before?" Alicia asked. "It's not easy."

"Our parents used to say it's one of the most difficult places in the world to catch fish," Pepedro added.

"Well, then it's a good thing I'm one of the world's greatest fishermen," Bobby answered. He held up his index finger, then skirted around us and climbed belowdecks. A few minutes later, he popped up, carrying a fishing rod and a tackle box. Then he stared at the rushing water. "The river's too fast here," Bobby said. "At this time of the day, I think we'll have more luck closer to the banks, where the fish are resting in the shade."

Alicia eyed the shore. "It would be too dangerous to steer the boat that close. We could get stuck in the shallows."

Crouching down, Bobby hovered in front of the plastic case holding the emergency life raft. "This is kind of an emergency, right?" he asked. But he didn't wait for us to answer.

Bobby pulled the case onto the deck, unsnapped a pair of metal clasps, and staggered back as it popped open like a clamshell. The rest of us moved away. The lid flipped back. A small engine folded out of the back, and a rough gray material inside began to expand, slowly taking the shape of a surprisingly large boat. The craft was long enough for Matt to lie down and stretch out. Two hard plastic benches unfolded and extended across the width of the raft. Within seconds, we had a fishing boat.

"Amazing," Pepedro said.

Bobby himself was staring in wonder.

Alicia poked at the hull. "Riverboats should be metal," she said. "The bottom of the Amazon is cluttered with trees and roots and sunken boats that reach right to the surface. They will tear a hole in this."

"Nah, this stuff is tough," Bobby insisted. "Nothing's going to rip through it." He crouched down and bit into the side of the boat. "See? Go ahead, take a bite."

Instead, I scratched at the sides. It felt like an air mattress. Ava checked the engine. "Electric?"

"It's the way of the world," Bobby said.

"Reminds me of the Snowgoer," Matt said quietly.

The Snowgoer, one of Hank's lesser-known inventions, is a four-passenger vehicle that's part snow blower, part bouncy house, mostly impractical, and completely fun.

He'd brought it down to Antarctica the previous year, and we'd used it to cruise over the ice. One bit of advice: if you're ever in a Snowgoer, don't take any jumps.

My brother leaned over the railing. His eyes were aimed at the river, but his thoughts were far away. I put my hand on his shoulder. "We'll find him," I whispered.

He nodded without looking up. "I know."

Bobby clapped his hands. "Who's coming with me to catch some dinner?"

Alicia wagged her finger. "I don't fish."

"I barely swim," Pepedro added.

Matt patted me on the back. "Jack will go with you."

Of course I would. My siblings cooked up the genius ideas. They mastered new languages and built satellites and robots. But someone had to jump through windows and climb into miniature boats on dangerous rivers.

Bobby clamped down on my shoulder. "What do you say, Jack-o?" he asked. "Are you ready to hook a monster? Maybe a pirarucu?"

"I'm ready to catch dinner," I said. "I don't care what it's called. Let's go."

Matt and Alicia lowered the boat into the water. I climbed in first. Bobby followed and shooed me to the bench at the bow. He flicked on the battery-powered motor, and we cut across the huge, wide river. The Amazon didn't flow in one steady direction. Some of the water rushed east, toward the sea. Some swirled in place. Boils and bubbles popped near the surface. Along the banks, huge branches and tree trunks rose up out of the muck. Here, the river flowed in the opposite direction, back toward the source of the waters, high in the Andes Mountains. The speed changed, too. The current was slow in some places and rapid in others.

The *Von Humboldt* was shrinking behind us. The boat swerved as Bobby steered around a tree limb drifting down the center of the river. I gripped the sides. The branch was racing past us like it had hidden propellers. I thought about what Alicia had said earlier—how entire boats were lying all over the river bottom, too. An entirely different world was hiding in that murky water.

115

"That's our pool right there," Bobby said, pointing to a swirling section of water beneath an overhanging tree. "See, Jack, you've got to think like a fish. And if I were a big old pirarucu, that's where I'd want to hang out."

The bow bounced as we sped across the river. Bobby threw a small anchor into the water, cut the engine, and netted a few dozen fat minnows. Then he readied his rod. He threaded his hook through the eyes of a still-wriggling fish about the size of two of my fingers and tossed it into the swirl. His cast was perfect. I watched the line for a minute, waiting for a monster to strike.

The first fish Bobby reeled in was small.

The second was smaller.

The third fish was only the size of my hand, and after Bobby flipped it into the bottom of the boat, he asked me to remove the hook. A year ago I would've refused, but I'd done a little fishing in Hawaii, so I was okay with handling the scaly swimmer. I grabbed a rag and held it still with one hand. But as I reached for the lure, the creature snapped at my fingers with a set of gnarly triangular teeth. I jumped back. "That's a piranha!"

My knowledge of these ter-rifying fish was limited to a few mentions in books and a movie about a mad scientist who devel-ops mutant piranhas with legs that swim to New York City and crawl around the streets at night,  attacking people as they came out of theaters and overturn-ing hot-dog carts to feast on boiled frankfurters. Sure, the little guy in the boat didn't have legs, but there was no way my fingers were going anywhere near those flesh-ripping, razor-sharp choppers.

"There are no piranhas in this part of the river," Bobby said, annoyed. "Just get the hook out."

I sat on my hands. "Nope. No way."

"Fine!" he shouted. "I'll do it myself!" He almost leaped out of the boat when the fish opened its mouth. "That's a piranha! Why didn't you tell me?"

Since Bobby wasn't going to touch the fish, either, he cut the line and tossed the miniature monster back into the river with the hook still embedded in its jaw. I wondered what happened when a creature was tossed back like that. Would he go tell his friends how he scared two humans? They'd probably think it was cool. Maybe they'd even consider attacking New York. For the hot dogs, at least.

The two fish Bobby had caught would barely feed one of us. So we motored up and down the river, anchoring in one supposedly perfect spot after another. We were out there for what felt like a couple of hours. Another meal of rice and beans no longer seemed all that bad. "Should we give up?" I asked.

"One last cast, Jack," Bobby said. "One last cast. Let's try another spot."

He steered the boat upriver and cruised around a giant tree sticking up out of the water like an enormous, bent finger, then signaled me to toss the small anchor. "We should probably stay away from that," I suggested.

Bobby ignored me. We swung downstream of the huge tree, and the hull bumped into something under the surface. A small tear opened in the bottom. Water flooded in

117

quickly. I tried covering the hole with my foot, but that only opened it more. "Bobby, we have a problem," I said. "There's a rip in the boat."

The *Von Humboldt* was nowhere in sight. We'd motored too far. My partner cheered. His rod was bending so much it looked ready to snap. "I've got a big one, Jack-O!" he shouted. "She's a beast!"

"The water's really coming in," I said.

"We're fine," he said. But he didn't even glance down. He held the rod with one hand and moved me aside. "Switch places. I need to move to the bow."

"Can I drive?"

"We're not going anywhere until I pull in this fish."

His reel wasn't turning. Whatever he'd hooked into didn't want to budge. Scientists discover new species in the Amazon all the time. One every three days, according to my brother. Mostly, they're tiny little guys. Frogs, insects—that sort of thing. But what if Bobby was about to pull up something entirely new? Ideally, our host would fall into the river at the last second. Then I'd grab his rod, reel in the creature, and get the credit. Would I get to name the new discovery? If so, I'd call it "the jackfish." There probably is a jackfish already, though. Maybe something more Amazonian would be better, like "the jackaru." Only if it was beautiful and majestic, though. If it was an ugly beast, I'd have to name it "the mattarando" or something.

Whatever creature was down there still wasn't giving up. And neither was Bobby. The water was up to our ankles but he didn't care. Sweat was pouring down his head. His eyes were turning red. Veins in his neck and arms were bulging. "Wipe my forehead!" he ordered.

Was he serious?

He asked me again. "No way," I answered.

"Please!" he shouted. "I can barely see."

And I couldn't see using my shirt to wipe some sweaty dude's face. So I grabbed the rag we'd used to hold the piranha. Bobby was sitting up in the bow, with his back to me. I worked fast, and he was grateful. Soon the fish scales would drip into his eyes, though. "We really should think about getting back," I reminded him.

The brown water was up to my shins. I started splashing it out of the boat. "Bobby, we seriously need to move," I said. "The river's coming in too fast. You have to release the fish."

"We're fine," he repeated.

I reached around him and started pulling up the anchor.

"I'm not giving up, kid," Bobby growled, his teeth clenched. "Leave that anchor alone." He grunted, unable to move the reel. "She's a fighter, but she'll tire soon, and we'll eat well."

119

Something about Bobby's voice was different. But I didn't have time to figure it out. The water was almost up to my knees. Bobby was standing now, pulling at the hidden creature with all his weight.

"I'm not sure you should be—"

"Quiet! I'm trying to concentrate!" he barked at me.

The piranha with the hook in his mouth was definitely circling in the water below. He'd probably called his buddies, too. They were all down there, waiting for us to sink. I looked back for the *Von Humboldt*, but the river curved, and a stand of trees leaning out over the water blocked our view of our friends.

"Almost got it!" Bobby yelled. "I can feel her getting weak."

And I was feeling the water rising faster and faster. The tackle box full of fishing lures was floating at my knees. Popping open the lid, I grabbed a knife, reached around Bobby, and slashed at the thin line. The rod snapped up toward the sky.

Bobby fell back and almost tumbled out of the boat.

Then he turned and grabbed me by the shirt. He started shouting and showering my face and shirt with angry spit. I crawled back toward the stern but he wouldn't let go. Honestly, he could've yelled me right off the boat into the river. And in the middle of all the screaming, I realized what was different about his voice.

His accent was gone. There was nothing Scottish or Irish about his voice. He sounded like any other American.

Suddenly he stopped yelling and looked all around him, as if he'd just woken from a dream to find himself in our half-sunken vessel. His legs were deep in the brown water. I was already soaked to the waist. We had minutes at most, and those piranhas were waiting. Maybe a furious jackaru, too.

Frantic, he moved to the back again, practically throwing me toward the bow. He started our engine, but the whirr of the motor faded quickly. "Dead," he said. "I hate batteries!" He pushed his hands back through his hair and squinted in the direction of the shore. "Can you swim?"

"Yes?"

"Is that a question or an answer?"

"I can swim. I just don't want to."

Bobby splashed at the water inside our boat. "This little vessel is going to go under in less than five minutes. Sorry, Jack, but we don't have a choice. We have to swim for shore."

I pointed to the submerged tree. "What about that? Can't we climb up onto that?"

"No way we're going to make that. We'd have to swim against the current."

The shore was just a few lengths of a pool away. Thin,

121

tall trees leaned out over the riverbank. The soil was the color of sand, and a few steps inland, green reeds and bushes and vines rose up like round and curving walls. The sunlight didn't penetrate that world of green. Shadows lurked everywhere. I thought I saw something move.

The bench at the bow was almost entirely underwater, but I sat anyway. I crossed my arms on my chest. "I'm not going anywhere."

Bobby sneered. "You'll make it. The current fades in strength once you get closer to shore, into the shallows."

"I'm waiting," I said. "They'll come looking for us."

"What's the matter? You afraid of a few fish?"

Yes. And I wasn't too thrilled about what might be waiting for us in those shadows, either. Not to mention that I trusted our captain about as much as a kid with his fingers crossed. If he'd been faking his accent this whole time, what else was he lying about?

"Go for it," I said. "I'm staying."

"Do what you like, Jack-o," Bobby said.

He lifted an arm over his head and pulled at the elbow. Then he did the same with the other arm. Bobby sucked in a few deep breaths, rolled his shoulders, and plunged headfirst into the water. The river swirled and rushed around our sinking boat. A river filled with sharp-toothed piranhas, deadly caimans, and menacing miniature fish.

Even the otters had sharp claws. And if none of those monsters managed to suck me under, the Amazon might do the job herself. If I didn't make it to the shore, the current would carry me out toward the Atlantic Ocean.

Really, there was only one choice.

I dove into the brown water.

Bobby was already a few body lengths ahead of me, swimming freestyle and kicking like a madman. I opted for doggy paddle. Or call it the capybara crawl. I stayed low, with just my mouth above the surface, and tried not to splash. That way, maybe the piranhas would be more attracted to Bobby—and I could hurry for shore while he was fending them off.

Something slick and rubbery brushed against my leg. Panicking, I thrashed at the water, then turned and swam backward. Whatever it was, the thing was huge. Had Bobby really hooked a legendary fish? And was it coming back for me now? I didn't even want to think about the other possibilities. The huge otters, for one. Or the beasts of the forest. One particularly terrifying jungle dweller liked slithering into the water in search of a snack. This monster didn't have deadly claws or teeth. Instead, it wrapped its victims in life-erasing hugs. And I really, really didn't want to be the next meal of a giant boa constrictor. I turned back onto my stomach. Forget the capybara crawl. I needed to

123

channel my inner Ava. I dropped my face into the water and swam as hard as possible.

The beast bumped my legs again.

And again.

My heart was pumping insanely fast. I churned and swung my arms and kicked with every muscle fiber in my skinny legs. Exhausted, completely out of air, I was almost too terrified to breathe. I picked up my head and wiped my eyes. The shore wasn't far. I could make it. I swam harder.

My hand hit something. Not a fish, though. And not a boa constrictor, either. My fingers dug halfway down into cool silt. The river bottom. I picked up my head. The actual shore was still thirty feet away, but I'd made it to the shallows, at least. The current had slowed. I kicked forward, then pulled my knees up under me. The water was waist deep. I stood and spun around, looking for the creature that had either been testing me as a possible meal or playing some weird Amazonian version of footsie. But I couldn't see anything through the latte-brown water. Still, there was no way I was turning around, either. Whatever it was that had bumped me was definitely coming back, and I needed to be able to see it. My heels sank into the mud as I backed up slowly, step-by-step, out of the running river.

"Stop," Bobby whispered behind me.

I twisted my head around. He was only a few strides from the shore, in water up to his knees, but he was crouching, holding his hands out to his sides. He turned his head only slightly as he spoke to me, keeping his eyes trained into the jungle. "Do not . . . come . . . any closer."

Slowly, I turned around completely. A large cat with spotted black-and-yellow fur was stepping silently out of the brush on padded paws. This was not the kind of feline that purrs and leaps onto bookshelves or pounces on little garden mice. This was one of the most feared predators in the jungle, a cat that could crush the skull of a capybara with a single snap of its powerful jaws.

Bobby was staring down a jaguar.

125

I turned sideways, watching the water for signs of the mystery creature while glancing at the slowly approaching predator. Bobby was backing toward me. "We're going to be okay," he said. His voice was calm and soothing. I actually believed him. "We're going to be fine, Jack." The jaguar was at the edge of the water. Bobby was nearly alongside me now, and his accent had returned. "Everything is going to be fine. But you're not in Brooklyn anymore, are you?"

The huge cat crawled closer.

"Are you sure we're okay?" I whispered.

Bobby laughed. "Yes, I'm sure. Because cats don't swim," he said, and he slapped his hand down across the face of the river, sending a huge splash toward the jaguar.

The creature growled.

Bobby pulled back his hand to splash it again, but I grabbed his forearm. "Please don't do that, Bobby," I said.

"Why not? That cat's not coming in here."

The jaguar stepped down into the river. "Here in the Amazon, cats swim," I said.

His face turned white. "Are you serious?"

The jaguar slowly entered the water, stepping toward us. Bobby cursed.

We heard the roar of an engine behind us. The *Von Humboldt* was cruising into view, spraying water in its wake. But neither of us moved. The river briefly became warmer. I looked at Bobby. He avoided my stare. He couldn't have. I mean, he was an adult. They didn't do things like that. Right?

Bobby started moving around me, walking up the river. "What are you doing?" I asked.

"I'm swimming back out," he said. "They won't be able to

get in this close, and we need to put as much water between us and that cat as possible."

"But there's something else out there," I warned him.

Bobby didn't listen. He ran upriver in the waist-deep water, plunged out into the current, and started swimming.

Now I was the jaguar's only prey.

I backed out into deeper water.

The creature was only fifteen feet away and inching closer.

Then it leaped up out of the water and splashed down only a few feet away. A wave of water rushed past me, knocking me onto my back. The river was swirling between me and the jaguar, as if we were suddenly caught in some kind of busted wave pool. Two strange pink forms cut through the surface. But they weren't snakes. The creatures had weird, ridged fins on their backs. The jaguar could still stand in the water, but it was slapping at the surface with its claws. The predator was panicking.

One of the enormous pink fish swung wide, kicked hard beneath the surface, charging the jaguar, and rammed it like some kind of underwater rhinoceros. The cat snarled. The second creature charged from the other side, slamming into the jaguar again. I kept backing into deeper and deeper water. The cat was almost out of the river now, growling back at the mysterious creatures hiding in the

127

murk. The beast wasn't even looking at me anymore. I could hear Matt and Ava calling to me. If I was going to try to make it out to the boat, this was my chance. I turned and swam blindly, furiously. When I finally looked up, the *Von Humboldt* wasn't far away. I buried my head and charged forward until I slammed my hand into its side.

Matt and Bobby pulled me, gasping, from the river, and I flopped onto one of the cushioned benches at the back, coughing out a gallon of water. My sister grabbed me by the arm and helped me up. "You're okay," she said. "You're okay."

I breathed. Bobby had already gone below. I stared back at the shore. The jaguar was slinking back into the brush. The strange pair of fish that had fought the creature had disappeared into the muddy water.

"You are okay, right?" Alicia asked.

"Yes, yes," I said. "What were those things?"

"Botos," Pepedro said with a smile. "You are very lucky. Not every tourist gets to see a boto. Not every fisherman gets rescued by one, either."

"What's a boto?" I asked.

"They're the pink dolphins," Ava explained.

"Not exactly," Alicia said. "They are maybe a different species." She held up her free hand. "They are very unique creatures. Some people believe they are magical creatures, citizens of the Encante, an underwater city beneath the river more beautiful than any kingdom on Earth. When people disappear in the river, they believe the botos have taken them to the Encante."

"Myths," Ava said. "People invent those stories to make themselves feel better when someone dies. They'd be better off accepting their deaths."

I'd heard Hank say something similar once. And I wondered if Ava really believed it.

"They also say that the botos can transform themselves into human form and make men and women fall in love with them. Maybe one of these botos liked you, Jack," Alicia added with a smile. "Maybe you'd like to marry one?"

Bobby climbed up from his cabin wearing a dry T-shirt and a new pair of purple lacrosse shorts. He tossed me a towel. He had another one wrapped around his neck. "Whoa! That was something, wasn't it, Jack?"

The lilt in his voice had returned; his accent was back. And I remembered that something else had been bothering me when we were facing the jaguar. But what?

"Are you serious?" Ava asked. "That was totally reckless. You both could have been killed."

"You didn't catch a fish, either," Pepedro added.

"I would have if little Jack here hadn't cut the line."

129

Little Jack? I was a few inches over five feet tall, thank you very much. That was thoroughly average for a kid my age.

"Besides," Bobby continued, "the important thing is that we survived because I was brave enough to swim away and force that jaguar to lose interest."

"But I—"

"Thank you," Bobby said. "That's all you have to say."

An army of intelligent robots with laser guns aimed at my chest couldn't have forced me to say those words. I stared at my sister. Subtly, she shook her head and mouthed the words "Let it go."

My clothes were soaked, and I smelled like dirty river water and fish scales. Down below, I washed my hands and face. While I was changing into dry clothes, a little clap of mental thunder rolled through my brain. Bobby's words on the shore came back to me.

But you're not in Brooklyn anymore, are you?

He knew we lived in Brooklyn, a detail we hadn't even shared with Dona Maria. He'd been faking his accent this whole time. He got the name of the boat wrong. He barely knew anything about the Amazon River. Or the rainforest. The guy didn't even know that jaguars could swim. And sure, this could have been a random coincidence, but given his lacrosse shorts, he seemed to like the color purple.

Bobby wasn't a captain.

He wasn't a river guide.

He was an impostor and a thief.

We had traveled all the way to Brazil to warn Hank about the crook who'd broken into his lab to steal his ideas. Now we were leading that man right to him.

9
DITCHING THE CAPTAIN

MY SIBLINGS DIDN'T NEED TO BE CONVINCED. BOBBY'S accent had been grating on Ava; the idea that he'd been faking it made perfect sense to her. Matt wondered how he'd discovered our plans, and I reminded him of the limo. The driver's phone was on speaker the whole time, and we'd discussed just about everything. Bobby had probably hired us the limo, then listened to our whole conversation. Ava guessed he'd been following us the whole time we were in Brazil.

"Do you think he got those kids to steal our phones?" my sister asked.

"No, they probably just stole them," Pepedro said.

Our supposed captain had gone below, and the Brazilians were checking occasionally to make sure he was still in his cabin. "We have to ditch him," Ava decided.

"Sure, but how?" I asked.

Matt was shaking his head. "We should've known! That first day, he didn't even ask our names."

"That's because we'd already met in Hank's lab," I said. "He knew all about us when he came looking for the drive."

Alicia signaled us to lower our voices.

"Okay," Ava said, "so what do we do now?"

Pepedro began juggling again, tapping the ball from one foot to the other, applying a little backspin with each flick. Without looking at us, he asked, "You think Bobby is traveling into the jungle just to get this drive?"

I shrugged. "It can't be a coincidence."

"Do you know if Hank still has it with him?" Pepedro asked.

"No, but he'd been carrying it everywhere," Matt said.

"In his little fanny pack, right?" Alicia asked. "I love this fanny pack. So American. But I still don't understand. Why so much trouble over some ideas?"

"Those ideas could be worth hundreds of millions of dollars," I explained.

"Oh," Alicia answered. "Then I would protect them, too. But maybe in something a little stronger than a fanny pack."

We heard Bobby's cabin door open, and Pepedro smothered the ball on the deck with the bottom of his foot.

"So then the proton replied, 'I'm positive,'" Matt said.

Ava fake-laughed and elbowed me. I forced a chuckle, then whispered to our confused Brazilian friends. "Science joke."

133

"Is it really this funny?"

"To them," I said.

Bobby smiled at us and returned to his perch at the bow. Ava switched on the stereo and turned up the volume. He turned around and gave us a thumbs-up.

"Can we hike from here?" Ava asked. "What if we leave tonight?"

"No," Alicia said. "We're not even close. We need to motor for at least two more days."

"So what do we do until then?"

"I don't know. Enjoy the Amazon?"

This was impossible. The river terrified me now. At night, the noises were only getting louder. I kept seeing the red eyes of caimans on the shore and imagining piranhas swimming beneath us and river otters sneaking onto the deck at night while we were in bed, then wriggling down to our bunks and tickling our faces with their huge, wet whiskers. I had a nightmare about marrying a boto. In the dream, my tuxedo was pretty sweet, but the sight of the dolphinlike creature in the white dress and veil shocked me awake, and I slammed my head on the bottom of Pepedro's bunk.

The rain was almost constant now, and Bobby became horribly bored. And when Bobby was bored, he liked simple card games best. The morning after our stare-down with the jaguar I played crazy eights with him for three hours.

134

After dinner that night, Matt and Ava were in the galley washing the dishes when I caught Alicia focusing on the shore. Bobby stood beside me, squinting in the same direction. "What are you looking at?" he asked her.

She coughed and smiled. "I thought I saw a jaguar, but it was nothing."

Later, at the door to our bunks, I caught up to her and whispered. "There was no jaguar, right?"

"There was no jaguar," she replied, her voice hushed. "We're here."

"Here? What do you mean? It has only been a day."

"There's another trail. But we have to leave tonight. Here, even when he finds us missing in the morning, the jungle will be too thick for him to track us."

After I passed along the message to my siblings, we quietly packed, then waited. Every fifteen minutes, Pepedro would creep out to see if Bobby was still awake. But he just wouldn't tire. At midnight he was still doing push-ups on the bridge. Not until one o'clock in the morning did we hear the door to his cabin click closed. We waited, and then Pepedro snuck into our rooms and told us it was time to leave.

On deck, the two Brazilians opened the plastic locker at the stern and pulled out two gleaming machetes. One more remained. I went to grab one. "No, no," Alicia said. "Not you."

135

"Why not?"

"You will accidentally chop off your hand."

"And you won't?"

"We were given machetes when we were six years old. We know how to use them."

"So do I," I said. I held out my hand and motioned for her to give it to me anyway. She passed me one of the blades. I swung it once and lost my grip. The blade flew across the deck and speared a life preserver.

If it were possible for one person to incinerate another with his eyes, Matt would have done so right then and there. For a moment we were silent, and I worried that I'd ruined everything. We listened. Thankfully, Bobby didn't stir. But I ruled out a possible career as a spy. Or a ninja.

Alicia quietly pulled the blade out of the life preserver and returned it to the locker. "No machete for you."

"Let's go before Jack wakes up the whole jungle," Ava suggested.

I swung my backpack up onto my shoulders. Ava did, too, and hers looked twice as stuffed. "Don't tell me you're bringing Betsy."

She shrugged. "I'm not leaving her here."

"Both of you will drop half that gear by tomorrow," Alicia predicted. "This is too much to carry through the Amazon."

She didn't know my sister.

Pepedro pointed to my high-tops. "You don't have boots?"

"He doesn't like boots," Ava said.

And she was right. "I'll be fine."

"You'll be wet," Alicia said.

After we'd checked and double-checked to make sure we had everything, Matt insisted on spraying Ava and me with some kind of organic insect repellent. A cloud of the stuff settled over us; I tasted it on my tongue and nearly vomited trying to keep down a cough. We climbed down onto the platform at the stern. The water was swirling behind the boat. Busted tree branches and dead leaves floated past in the current. Alicia leaned over and grabbed a stick the length of a baseball bat and broke off a few thin offshoots. She quietly lowered herself into the river and held her backpack on one shoulder. The water was stomach deep. As she walked, she poked at the river bottom with the stick.

My brother followed her. "What are you doing?" he asked.

"Sometimes there are sting rays in the sand," Pepedro explained. "They leave you sore for a week."

"Get me a stick," Ava said. "Please."

The water was warm, and we copied Alicia, holding our bags out of the river. The music of the jungle was getting

137

louder with each step. The bugs and birds and maddening monkeys buzzed and shrieked and blared. Thick clouds blocked the moonlight. The shore was only twenty paces away. "Where's the path?" I asked.

Ava told me to be quiet.

My high-tops were squelching into the silt. Was it a good idea to insist on wearing basketball sneakers instead of hiking boots? No, probably not. I definitely wasn't going to win a Nobel Prize for the decision. But I was committed now.

"We should have taken our shoes off first," Matt said.

"There's no use," Pepedro said. "This is the Amazon rainforest. Your shoes will be wet every minute of every day."

138

Alicia was walking toward a dense thicket of wide, green, waxy leaves. I checked behind me for botos. Alicia said they often visited humans in the middle of the night, and I really wasn't up for marrying a dolphin. The thick jungle in front of us didn't exactly look welcoming, either. "What about jaguars?"

"The cats will not want to bother us," said Pepedro. "We are too many."

"What about snakes?" Matt asked.

Ava scanned the trees. "Or vampire bats?"

Part of me was glad to hear the geniuses were nervous, too. But our guides didn't exactly swat our fears away.

They didn't say anything at all. Alicia reached forward and pushed aside the wide leaves. Following a step behind her, Matt slipped on the muddy riverbank. He reached up and grabbed a branch to stop himself from falling. The rain and dew on all the leaves flooded down, dousing him. Normally I would've laughed. Instead I grabbed him by the elbow. He nodded, thanking me, and followed Alicia into the brush.

"You might want to duck," she warned.

We did, but it barely helped. The leaves slapped against our faces and swept across our backs, soaking us through our clothes. Ever wonder what it would be like to walk through one of those automatic car washes? Now I think I know.

There was a tiny clearing a few paces ahead. The space was barely large enough to fit the five of us. "This is it," Alicia said. "Are we ready?"

We tightened our backpacks.

"This is the trail?" Matt asked.

He stood up straight and bumped his head on a branch. Wet, waxy leaves pushed into the side of my face like the hands of some creepy jungle monster. Something screeched so loud it felt like the creature was yelling directly into my brain. Crickets or cicadas buzzed like a million violinists playing busted instruments. A distant roar rolled through the jungle and shook me to my bones. Hank had gotten us into a Coldplay concert once. We'd stood near a Matt-size set of speakers. After that night, my ears rang for two days. But the concert was nothing compared to the jungle. The rainforest was easily the loudest place I'd ever been in my life.

My brother slapped himself in the face. "Ow!" Matt shouted. "Something just bit me!"

"Get used it," Pepedro replied. "And be quiet. We're still close to the boat."

Alicia laughed and pushed ahead. "Follow me."

"Where?" Ava asked. "I don't even see a path!"

"There is a kind of path," Pepedro replied. "Welcome to a Trilha da Dor."

"What does that mean?" I asked.

"I don't actually know," Ava admitted.

"A Trilha da Dor," Pepedro explained, "means the Trail of Pain."

10
THE TRAIL OF PAIN

WHEN I SCRAPE OR CUT MY LEG, SOMEONE ELSE usually notices first. I rarely cry at the dentist. Needles? I don't even flinch. One time someone threw a football at me so hard that it knocked my finger out of joint, and I barely cried when my foster dad popped it back into place. Generally, I consider myself to be pretty tough.

Then I discovered the Trail of Pain.

Forget the car wash comparison. Walking through the rainforest at night combined about seventeen different kinds of torture. Leaves and branches and thorny limbs snapped against my face, chest, and arms. I stepped on a rotten log and a horde of ants crawled over my shoe. In a rush I swept them away, but a dozen of them still clamped their tiny little jaws into my skin, biting me through my socks, and it felt like a hundred wasps were stinging me at once. Invisible flies dug into my neck and ankles. Even the supposedly protected spots were open to their attacks. Yep: something bit me on the butt. How does that even happen? Great question. It's not like I was walking around mooning the monkeys.

Oh, and speaking of monkeys—they were beyond loud. According to Matt, the howlers were the loudest land animals on the planet. They typically swung around in groups of fifteen or twenty monkeys, too, so their roars sounded like armies stampeding toward us through the jungle.

My sneakers were soaked through. My socks were like warm, wet washcloths, and even though it was the middle of the night, I was sweating. Plus our two guides weren't even using their ridiculously cool machetes. They hadn't hacked away a single leaf, and I had to walk with my arms out in front of me, blocking branches like a karate master fending off kicks. Once or twice I might have added a quiet little *"Hi-yah!"*

Meanwhile, Alicia was humming, Pepedro whistling. Both of them said a few times how it felt so good to be back. I was just ahead of Pepedro, and we'd been hiking for hours when I finally gave up. I swatted at least seven flies on my neck and ankles, leaned forward for a breath, and crouched. "We need to stop."

The boy with the million dollar foot patted me on the back. "We've only been walking for an hour, Jack."

"Seriously?" my brother asked.

At least he was exhausted, too.

142

"I'm fine," Ava said.

Of course she was.

Alicia tapped her watch. The face glowed green. "We have not been walking for an hour, either. It has only been sixteen minutes," she said. "We need to put as many kilometers between us and the boat as possible. Our friend Bobby could catch us if we're too slow."

"Could you at least use your machetes?" I asked.

"No," Pepedro replied.

"You can't leave a trail, right?" Ava guessed.

"That's right," Alicia said. "He could track us."

"Maybe you could ease up on the whistling?" Matt suggested. "I don't mean to be rude, but it's kind of annoying."

"You don't want me to stop whistling," Pepedro said.

"No?"

"You're not the only one who doesn't like that sound," Alicia said. "It keeps certain creatures away."

All three of us started whistling right along with them. As we trudged through the jungle, Pepedro would occasionally grab a handful of leaves or break off a branch, then reach over his shoulder and stuff them into his backpack. I tried to stay focused on what was right in front of me: the ground; the branches snapping back from the person ahead. When Pepedro pointed out an interesting creature or plant, I'd jot down a few facts in my notebook. The pages were damp from the mist, the ink was running, and there was barely enough light to see my pen on the page. But if I didn't write these things down, I might never remember them.

The bugs and biting flies were cosmically annoying, but I couldn't help thinking about how they were just a few of the creepy, crawling, stalking dangers of the jungle. That jaguar, for instance. Maybe she really had followed us up the river. A golden lancehead snake, one of the fastest and deadliest in the world, could've been slithering nearby. At any second, a herd of furious peccaries could have stampeded through, goring us with their tusks. Maybe a really angry toucan wanted to peck us with his giant beak. Or an anteater. Their claws were so sharp, and their arms so strong, they could rip open a jaguar's stomach.

Every few minutes I shook my head, trying to clear out all these thoughts. And we kept walking. The next few hours felt like a few days. My eyes stung from the mix of sweat and bug spray dripping down from my brow. The whistling became as familiar as my breathing. As we walked and crawled and climbed over wet tree limbs and fallen, decaying branches and trunks, pushing away thick leaves, swatting constantly, blocking limbs that recoiled like slingshots when the person in front of you let go, my brother and sister were using their laser pointers to highlight cool bugs and creatures. Every so often, Pepedro stopped us, too. Once, he pointed to these weird, Hershey's Kiss–shaped growths all around the trunk of a giant tree. Matt leaned forward to touch one, but Pepedro grabbed his hand. "Careful," he warned. "They sting."

"Even the trees sting?" Ava asked.

"Here in the jungle, almost everything stings," Pepedro said. "But the jungle provides for you, too, if you know her secrets." He raised his eyebrows at a vine dangling off to my right. He grabbed it with two hands, then snapped it. A thin stream of clear liquid rushed out. Pepedro leaned over, tilted his head, and drank. Then he passed me the vine. "Go ahead," he said. "It's just water."

Maybe that was true, but it was warm and tasted like bark. I sipped, then passed it to Matt. "Try some. It's delicious."

As I hurried ahead to catch Pepedro and Alicia, I heard Matt spitting it out. Soon my thoughts started following another weird current. Normally, I tried to set limits to my mind drifts, like hooking your dog to a long leash in the backyard. But now I let the random thoughts roll and started wondering what sort of creature I'd want to be in the rainforest. A vampire bat? A boa constrictor? The howler monkeys had amazing beards. It would be fun to yell all the time, too. Being small, like a fly, would be cool. But then you'd have so many annoying brothers and sisters. And

145

you'd only live for a few days at most. Or what if I were a Brazilian free-tailed bat? On the plane, I'd read that they were the fastest fliers in the world.

"Jack," Ava whispered. "Pepedro's talking to you."

Our guide pointed to something clinging to a nearby tree limb. I figured he was pointing out another strange plant. Then I realized what was lurking behind the leaves in front of me. A hairy, glorious, and completely mellow sloth. I could barely see the little guy in the moonless dark. He was leaning away from the tree, slowly turning his gaze our way, and I loved him immediately. A bunch of weird humans were stomping through his neighborhood and he barely bothered to look. Nothing was going to stress out a sloth. Let everyone else in the jungle slither and swing, scream and roar. This dude just chillaxed.

Forget the bat. If I had to choose, I'd be a sloth.

Matt stopped between Ava and me. "Do you know that as many as a thousand beetles can live in a sloth's fur?"

"That's gross," I said.

"I think it's cool," Ava said. "What's it doing?"

"Going to his bathroom," Matt guessed. "Once a week,

the sloth comes down to the ground, digs a little hole, relieves itself of the week's food, and climbs back up again."

Ava thought that was fascinating. And sure, I still worshipped the creature. Even with all the beetles in its hair. But I didn't need to watch it make a jungle toilet. "Let's go," I said. "Alicia's still moving."

When we finally reached our first campsite, my hopes soared, then belly flopped. A tree with a base as wide as a car rose up in the center of the small clearing. The space was only about ten giant steps across. "I was expecting . . ."

"Tents?" Alicia asked with a smile. "Maybe little barbecues?"

"A shelter would have been nice," Ava said.

"The jungle would swallow it in two weeks," Alicia said. "Even the trail and this clearing are little miracles. Our parents used to walk this path once a month."

"They hiked the Trail of Pain every month?" I asked.

"For them, it was not painful," Alicia said. "For them, it was fun."

She stared at the jungle floor. After a moment, Pepedro put his arm around his sister's shoulders, and we knew enough to be quiet and wait.

Alicia wiped her eyes. "Okay, let's set up."

I looked around at the weeds and vines, then up at the towering tree. "Where do we even lie down?"

"We don't lie down," Alicia said. "We go up."

She removed a rope hammock from her backpack, climbed the tree, then strung the woven bed along a limb as thick as a softball and tied several complex knots. Hank was weirdly obsessed with knots, and he'd tried to teach me a few of them. "Is that a timber hitch?" I asked.

"I don't know," she said. "It's a knot."

She draped a mosquito net over the limb so it hung down over the hammock, then climbed around the trunk to the next strong limb. Pepedro scaled the tree on the opposite side and started stringing up another makeshift bed. Alicia called for our hammocks.

"Tonight we'll help you because we have only a few hours until sunrise and we have to move fast," she said. "Tomorrow night you can make your own bed."

They advised us to tie our backpacks up in the tree, too. Otherwise they'd be covered with bugs in the morning. Once her hammock was set up, Ava climbed the tree, squeezed in, and wished everyone a good night.

"Should we set an alarm?" Matt asked.

"You will not need an alarm," Pepedro said with a laugh.

The hammock was actually comfortable, even though a hundred thin ropes were digging into my back. By the time I settled into my swinging bed and pulled the thin mosquito net around me, Ava was snoring. But Matt was strangely chatty. The tree canopy formed a leafy ceiling that blocked our view, and he was saying how weird it was to sleep outside and not see the sky or stars. I've been trying to cut back on my *Star Wars* references, since Hank is more of a *Star Trek* guy, but sleeping up in that tree, I kind of felt like an Ewok. Only not quite so furry. And with better teeth.

My brother was droning on about the different stars in the Southern Hemisphere when I remembered the earplugs the guy had given me on the plane. My backpack was hanging within arm's reach. I found them in a side pocket and popped them in. Matt's lecture faded to a whisper, and morning arrived about five minutes later, as I awoke to the growls and roars of distant howler monkeys. Apparently, the earplugs weren't totally jungle proof. I removed them and shoved them in my pocket. Matt was already in the middle of a new lecture. Either that, or the one from the night before had never stopped. This time, though, he was talking about the monkeys, and how their morning shouts were a way of declaring their territory. I stretched.

Apparently, I wasn't the only one bored with Matt's chatter. A large, gray monkey was perched on a branch high above him. I thought he was just watching us. Matt probably did, too. He was pointing at the hairy dude. But the monkey wasn't observing us, exactly. He had other plans.

A stream of liquid flowed down and splashed off the trunk near my brother. Matt lost it. He screamed, then drew his legs in close to avoid getting sprayed.

His hammock swung, and my brother fell out. He grabbed his rope bed before he hit the ground, then hung there for a second before dropping the last few feet.

A few last bursts splashed off the tree.

Then the monkey was done.

My brother was safe.

And I was ready to give in to what was going to be one of the greatest laughing fits of my life. But then I turned to the opposite side of my hammock and froze.

A scaled, bright green snake was wrapped around the limb to my right. Its body was as thick as my leg, and it was coiled several times around the branch. The creature had to be at least ten feet long. Slowly, it slid along and extended its head toward me. The white patches on its skin looked like computer pixels. The dark vertical slits in the snake's cold gray eyes were staring right at me. But I couldn't remember what kind of snake it was and whether it was deadly. "Matt," I whispered. "Enough about the monkeys. We have a problem."

"What's the . . . whoa! Don't move, Jack!"

"I wasn't planning on it. Maybe you could lower your voice a little?"

The snake moved its head right, then left, like it was studying me from different angles. Sometimes I did the same thing with cheeseburgers. Was I this creature's next meal?

"You're fine," Ava said from below. "That's an emerald tree boa. They're not venomous."

"You're sure?"

Alicia was standing below me now. "Stay still, Jack."

"But it's not dangerous, right?"

She didn't answer.

The snake extended itself, closing the space between us. I was close enough to tickle the thing. Then its jaws opened wide, revealing a set of teeth that made a piranha's choppers look as harmless as a plastic comb. I screamed.

The creature's head fell. Its body untangled from the limb, and it dropped toward the forest floor, right onto Pepedro's shoulders. Alicia grabbed the other end of the snake, and the two of them carefully lowered it to the ground.

"What happened?" Ava asked.

For a second I wondered if my scream had paralyzed the monster. Did I have a hidden superpower?

Pepedro held up a thin wooden blowgun. "Just knocked her out," he said.

"Where did you get that thing?" Matt asked.

"I carry it with me," Pepedro said with a shrug.

"Enough about the blowgun," I said. "Ava, you told me they weren't dangerous!"

"I said they weren't venomous," she explained. "Those teeth looked pretty serious, though."

Pepedro laid the snake in the cover of a bush and backed away. "You would have been fine," he said. "These snakes eat fat little rodents, not skinny Americans."

My hand was shaking as I reached to grab the limb above me. I crawled out of my hammock, stood on the limb below, and untied my hanging bed. Then I grabbed my pack and scurried down the tree. The snake hadn't moved. But when that thing awoke, I was sure he was going to come for me. Maybe the piranhas would join him, along with a couple of otters and a boto in a wedding dress. "Let's get going," I said.

"Are you okay?" Pepedro asked. "You're itchy?"

Without realizing it, I was furiously scratching my shoulder. My forearms were covered with welts, and my ankles itched so badly I wanted to chop them off. I crouched and dug my nails into the skin. Pepedro told me to stop, then he ripped a thick leaf from a small tree a few steps away. He snapped the leaf in half, revealing a sticky, oozing goo. "Hold out your hands," he said. I did, and he squeezed a huge clump of the goo into my palms. "Rub that on the bumps."

153

The stuff looked like alien mucous, but I was desperate. I slathered it all over my ankles, my wrists, the back of my neck. Then I smeared some straight across the top of my forehead. The goo dried quickly. My skin felt like it was covered with a thin layer of paper. But the itch . . . the itch was completely gone.

"It's okay?" Pepedro asked.

"It's amazing!" I said.

"The Amazon has many wonders."

Once we'd packed our hammocks, we didn't stretch or linger. We just started marching. Since we'd put enough distance between ourselves and the boat, Alicia and Pepedro were finally swinging their machetes. The bugs were still nipping, but at least I wasn't getting slapped in the face and chest with leaves and branches. Packing high-tops instead of hiking boots was probably one of the worst decisions I'd ever made. But I couldn't admit it. I kept telling Matt and Ava that my sneakers were great, and that they probably should've followed my lead. Every so often, our guides would grab fruit from a tree and order us to do the same. Their version of a fast-food breakfast, basically.

Late that night, we stopped again in a clearing that looked like the first one. Matt wondered aloud if it was the first one, but Alicia and Pepedro assured us that we were not lost. "How do you know?" Ava asked.

"Are you tracking the changes in the foliage?" Matt asked.

Ava held up her index finger. "Or tiny variations in air pressure?"

Pepedro laughed. "No, she's following these," he said, pointing to the trunk.

Two diagonal, parallel marks had been slashed into the bark with a machete. Alicia traced them with her fingers. "Our parents made them."

Stringing up our own hammocks was way harder than I'd expected. And I don't know if it was intentional or accidental, but Matt, Ava, and I ended up on one side of the tree and Pepedro and Alicia on the other. My sister and I were close enough to reach each other, and Matt was just below us. For a while, after settling into our woven beds, we were quiet. The Brazilians were breathing heavily. I figured my siblings were asleep, too, and I was getting ready to pop in my earplugs.

Then Matt spoke, his voice just louder than a whisper. "Do you think he's okay?"

"You mean alive?" Ava asked.

"Yeah, I guess so," Matt replied. "I'm sure he's fine. I mean, he's been through much worse, right?" He paused. Was he waiting for us to reassure him? He was the older one. That was supposed to be his job. "I just . . . I don't know."

The jungle was unusually quiet, as if it were waiting for us to finish.

155

"He's fine," Ava insisted. "We're going to find him and he's going to be fine."

That night I enjoyed a deep, heavy slumber filled with unusual dreams. The giant river otters were playing the monkeys in a soccer match, using their wide tails to kick, and heading in several goals with surprising accuracy. They might have had a dance contest, too, and I think there was a princess involved. I can't remember the entire dream, but I do know that I woke up as thirsty as a dog after a long walk. At first, I hardly moved. I turned my head slightly, looking left, then checked my right side, and the space above me. No snakes. Already the day was off to a better start.

When I removed my earplugs, I heard Matt snoring and the howler monkeys roaring. None of them were close enough to pee on our heads, though. I wanted a shower, but not that kind. Ava was sleeping with her mouth open slightly, making little purring noises, and a monkey with a glorious gray moustache was perched in a neighboring tree, staring at me. I yawned. Then I carefully climbed down. Pepedro and Alicia had already packed their hammocks. Their backpacks were gone, too, and I didn't hear or see either of them. They hadn't left us before. We'd barely ever been out of their sight. Immediately I started to panic. My heartbeat quickened. My breathing shortened.

At the edge of the clearing, I stood and listened to the strange music of the rainforest: the swaying leaves above, the light rain, the distant roars, the songs of birds and insects. Then, in the middle of that mad concert, I heard voices. Rough, deep voices that sounded nothing like our friends.

11
LASER ASSASSIN

OMEONE LAUGHED. MY FEAR TURNED TO HOPE. WAS IT Hank? Had they found him? I checked on my siblings. Matt was still snoring. Ava was out, too. And I had an awesome idea. I'd hurry into the jungle, grab Hank, and bring him back here while they were still sound asleep. They'd be totally surprised.

The laughter stopped. But it hadn't come from far away. I crept through the jungle, staying low. The voices weren't getting any clearer, but I still heard them ahead of me. Through the trees I heard the quiet roar of moving water. Not a river, though. The sound was more like a waterfall. That would have been just like Hank, to find some hidden paradise in the middle of the terrifying jungle. I wouldn't have been surprised if he'd built himself a little vacation hut on the edge of the waterfall. He was probably sitting there making coffee.

The wind shifted. No, not coffee. Something even better. The lip-smacking, stomach-soothing smell of roasted meat was drifting toward me through the thick, wet air. They said

Hank had switched back to being a carnivore. The only thing better than waking Matt to the sight of our mentor would be dangling a freshly charred drumstick above his nose while he was sleeping. And maybe convincing another monkey to relieve itself on the tree.

I started to run, ignoring the leaves slapping my face, yanking away the vines that hooked onto my arms. The roar of the water was growing louder and louder, and the voices were changing, too. Someone laughed again, but it definitely wasn't Hank's laugh. I reached forward, hoping to sweep away the branches in front of me, but my hands grabbed empty space. My right heel slid down a muddy bank. I dropped, sliding into a river spilling over a wide rock ledge. The swirling current pushed me off my feet and swept me forward.

The water was rushing over the top of a small waterfall. I tried to grab something to stop myself. But I was rolling, tumbling along the bottom. My right side bumped into a huge rock, and the water carried me up and over and then down. The drop was quick; I didn't even think to breathe. The water drove me down into a churning pool of cool green. My left side slammed down into a rock at the bottom. The water kept pounding me from above, pinning me, and I desperately needed to breathe. Then my mind cleared. I rolled, set my feet on the rock, and pushed off at an angle.

The pool wasn't too deep. I burst to the surface sooner than I'd expected and gasped for air. The water was swirling all around me. Head down, I swam hard for the closest bank. My hands grabbed two tufts of overgrown grass and weeds, and I kicked forward to get myself up out of the water.

Two rough hands clamped around my skinny wrists and yanked me up onto the riverbank. I flopped down and lay there for a second with my eyes closed. The hands that had grabbed me were not the hands of a scientist. The foul stench of a flaming cigar hung in the air, mingling with the roasting meat. A man shouted in Portuguese. His voice was gravelly.

I rolled over, opened my eyes, and held up my hands. My whole body ached. He pressed his boot against my ribs and pushed. "Please," I muttered.

The man was burly and bearded and his face was scattered with red marks and welts. The muscles in his jaw suggested he chewed rocks instead of gum. A small fire burned behind him. Another man, short and thin and brown-skinned, stood by the flames, where a pig roasted on a handmade wooden spit. The bearded man kept shouting at me in Portuguese. He held his boot above my stomach like he was going to stomp on me.

I tucked in my elbows to protect my ribs, covered my stomach with my forearms, and yelled back, "*No hablo Español!*"

The bearded man was suddenly silent.

The waterfall roared behind me.

The smaller, thinner man stepped forward. "American?" he asked. I nodded. "Why did you just tell us you don't speak Spanish? We are in Brazil. They speak Spanish over there—" he paused, thinking for a moment, then pointed back over his left shoulder "—in Argentina and Chile."

Right. Of course. I was kind of glad Matt and Ava hadn't heard that. But I was being threatened by strange men in the middle of the rainforest. How was I supposed to get my languages straight?

I coughed. There was a faint taste of bile in the back of my mouth. "Please, I'm sorry. No offense."

The thin man tilted his head and squinted. "How did you get up here? What are you doing in the middle of the jungle?" He caught me staring at the mud-encrusted, wide-toed, rib-crushing brown boot of his partner. "He will not hurt you, okay?" I nodded. Then, slowly, I crawled to a sitting position. The thin man crouched before me. "I ask you again, how did you get here?"

I had to think quickly. That doesn't always work out for me. "I was in a plane with my parents," I started. The bearded man moved away, walking over to the fire. Their bags were open. Some of their gear was spread out on a small mat. A partially folded map was sticking out the top of one

161

of their backpacks. "We were on vacation," I continued. "In the middle of the night, our plane was struck by lightning. All the plane's navigation systems were fried. We were about to crash when my mother reached over and pulled the ejection lever on my seat." I stopped and lifted my hands to cover my face. Then I performed a few fake sobs, wiped my nose, and continued. "I flew into the air like a rocket. It was so cold," I said, hugging myself as if I were frigid. "I was in shock, and I thought I was doomed, but then my parachute opened. I still wasn't safe, though."

"No?"

The bearded man removed a small canvas bag from inside his backpack. A logo with the letters *SA* was sewn into the backpack straps. I'd seen that logo before. But where? The man was watching the trees on the opposite bank as he pulled out what looked like a gun. Ava. Matt. Alicia and Pepedro. Please be safe, I thought. Please don't be hiding out there trying to rescue me.

I closed my eyes. This story had to work. I had to focus. "No, not yet," I continued. "The parachute had opened too low. It wasn't slowing down. I crashed through the trees. Something must have hit me in the head, because I was knocked out. When I awoke, my parents were gone, and I couldn't find any trace of the plane."

While his partner scanned the opposite bank with the

gun resting on his knee, the thin man watched me through narrowed eyes. The squinting, the creases in the forehead—they reminded me of these faces Hank made whenever I tried to convince him that I wasn't sending prank e-mails from his address. The man's right eyebrow rose higher than its neighbor. He started nodding. "Yes, yes," he said. "I know your story well. After you lost your parents, you wandered for many days, but then you found your way to a hidden city in the middle of the jungle, built by humans and maintained over the centuries by intelligent monkeys, yes?"

"Well, except for the—"

"This is the plot of *Monkey Boy*! You think I'm stupid?"

Okay. So in my rush to come up with a story, I'd totally summarized the beginning of that movie I'd watched on the plane. "The monkeys weren't that intelligent."

"The movie was not, either," said the man. "It is a complete rip-off of *The Jungle Book*, the story about the boy Mowgli."

"Yes, but I liked the part—"

"Quiet! We are not going to debate the plots of bad movies. You will tell me how you got here, and who you are with, or my friend Roger will kick you in the ribs."

"His name is Roger?"

The skinny man muttered to his bearded partner, who pulled his foot back like he was going to blast a soccer ball

163

into a distant goal. "Okay, okay!" I yelled. "I'll tell you!" Roger stopped and set his boot on the ground.

"Who is here with you? And do not tell me about monkeys."

I coughed. My arm ached from slamming into the rock. I'd probably get battered if I told him I was wandering through the rainforest with two teenage geniuses, a young sports agent, and a boy with a million dollar foot. "My parents," I said. "We weren't in a plane crash. We're exploring. My dad, he's a scientist, and my mom, she's Japanese, but she doesn't know karate or anything."

Without thinking, I'd described Hank and Min. But why? I'd always pictured my parents as fabulously good-looking business tycoons who dressed in designer clothes and had perfect hair all the time, even when they were driving around in their matching Teslas.

The thin man stomped. His wide brow creased. "Do you think I am some kind of racist? Why would I assume she knows karate?"

"No, I just—"

"Alex, shh!" Roger pointed into the jungle near the top of the waterfall. He whispered.

"Your names are Alex and Roger?"

"Quiet! Something moved," Alex said. He grabbed my

T-shirt at the chest and pulled me close. His breath smelled like a mix of salt and feet. "Who are you with?"

"Watch out, Mom!" I shouted. "He's got a gun!"

Alex grabbed the back of my neck and shoved me down into the thick grass. If I hadn't turned my head at the last second, my nose would have shattered. Then Alex let go. He backed away.

"Roger!" he whispered.

The bearded man grunted. Alex pointed to his partner's chest. A small red laser dot was moving around just below his chin. They both stared into the forest on the opposite side of the river, searching for the source. Roger dropped his gun, held up his hands, and shouted in Portuguese. The whole scene was weirdly familiar. Not the waterfall or the campfire, exactly, but the lasers. Then I remembered. *Sniper Assassin.* Matt wasn't sleeping. He was using his laser pointer to trick Roger into thinking someone had a rifle aimed at his chest just like the hero in the movies.

Now Roger looked over at Alex. Still holding his arms high, he pointed. A red dot was dancing around on Alex's forehead. Ava's laser pointer, most likely.

Alex draped his arm across my chest and held me up like a human shield. Then he grabbed the gun off the ground and pressed it into my neck. The blood rushed from my head. My jaw tingled. I couldn't feel my hands or legs, but everything was suddenly cold, and then the jungle around me, the rushing green water, the slowly roasting pig, the two frightening men—all of it disappeared.

I awoke on my back, staring up at the overhanging trees. A light rain was falling on my face. I heard voices, people crashing through the jungle. Slowly, I rolled onto my side. Alex was gone. Roger, too. And they hadn't even paused long enough to grab their packs. I grabbed the laminated map, folded and stuffed it into my pocket, then jumped into the river.

My feet sank into the grassy, weed-covered bottom. The current swept me away, but the water was barely three feet deep and no wider than a public pool. Compared to the Amazon River, it felt like a stream. I ran across, pulling with my arms, and didn't waste time looking for any creatures. This wasn't caiman country. Or at least I hoped not. And I didn't think piranhas would be in this little river, either. But I was pretty sure there were snakes. Still, I wasn't staying on the same side of the river as the angry dudes with the gun.

Downstream, a tree leaned over the water. The bank had been washed away, exposing roots as thick as Matt's arms. I let the river carry me closer, then dove for one of the roots. The river swept my legs out from under me, but I managed

167

to get one knee up onto the bank. Then I pulled myself out of the water, rolled into the brush, and scrambled through the jungle like a hunted pig, only without the snorting. Or the short, bristly hairs. The ground sloped up. That had to mean I was going the right way, back toward the top of the waterfall.

Once the ground leveled out again, I stopped and breathed. But I didn't have long to rest. Something large was crashing through the jungle, heading straight for me. A jaguar, maybe. Or one of the giant wild boars. I grabbed the nearest weapon without looking and got ready to defend myself. The beast was nearly on top of me when I blindly lashed out.

"Oww! That was my eye!"

The beast was my brother. He was blinking.

"Sorry? I thought you were a jaguar."

"Then why'd you slap me with a leaf?"

I looked down at the weapon in my hand. Had I really grabbed a leaf? Yes, and a wet one, too. "Sorry, I—"

He grabbed my shirt at the shoulder. "Shh! Let's go. Follow me."

Matt found his way back to our campsite, where Alicia, Pepedro, and Ava were hurriedly packing all our gear.

"Jack! That trick of yours was brilliant!"

"Trick?"

"Pretending to faint," Alicia said. "Ava said it's one of your gifts."

My sister was staring into her pack, hiding her smile. "Yes, well, you know . . ."

Ava tossed me my backpack and my unrolled hammock.

"What did you think of the laser pointers?" Matt asked.

"Genius," I said. "I told you those movies were good."

Matt bowed. "Definitely better than they looked."

"Who were those guys?" Ava asked.

Pepedro held his hand out flat and lowered it toward the forest floor. "We should keep our voices low, okay? They will start to look for us soon. As for who they are, we don't know," he said. "I smelled their fire this morning. We thought it might be Hank, so Alicia and I went to go see."

"Are they hunters?" Ava asked.

"No one hunts here."

I pulled the map out of my pocket and threw it to Alicia. "I grabbed this."

Alicia unfolded the laminated map and spread it out on the ground. The whole thing was as wide as one of my forearms and shaded green, with winding rivers marked in blue. There were red markings all over the map, too. Someone had been circling areas with a Sharpie. Certain regions were shaded with parallel lines, others marked with an *X*. The logo in the lower left corner matched the one I'd seen on Roger's canvas bag. "Do you know what that stands for?" I asked.

"Yes, and we should have known," she said. "They are scouts for a logging company. The *SA* stands for 'Super Andar.'"

"Where have I seen it before?"

"A billboard in the city, maybe?" Pepedro suggested.

"Andar means floor, right?" Ava asked.

"Yes," Alicia said. "Super Floor is a very big lumber company. Of course they would never admit to destroying the rainforest. Instead, these companies hire scouts to go into the jungle to inspect the trees, and if the forest looks promising, if the trees are tall and straight"—she nodded to a towering, powerful kapok steps from where we'd slept the previous night—"like this one here, they send crews to cut them down and fly in helicopters to pluck the trees from the jungle like a child picking flowers from a garden."

My sister started to reply. "That is so—"

Pepedro clasped her shoulder and pointed into the brush. "Shh!" he whispered. "They're coming back."

The four of them crouched and crowded behind me. I hurried to the back and pushed Matt to the front. He was the largest, after all. "Should we run?" I asked quietly.

Something moved ahead of us, to the left.

A man half-covered in leaves leaned out from behind a tree. His face was smeared with mud. He wore green pants and a camouflage jacket. He should have been smiling. But Hank Witherspoon was staring at us like we were visitors from Mars.

171

12
WHAT HAPPENS IN ASPEN

Okay, so that wasn't a great example. Matt and Hank would probably remind me that even if there were life on Mars, it would be tiny. The kind of thing you can only see through a microscope; nothing human-shaped or -sized. Anyway, my point was that he was completely surprised. Which was natural, really. We were supposed to be back in Brooklyn. Instead, we were deep in the Amazon rainforest. "What are you doing here?" he whispered.

Matt was moving toward him. Looking for a one-armed guy hug, I guessed. But then my brother stopped. "Well," he said, "we were—"

"Never mind," Hank said, cutting him off. Then he pointed at my shoes. "You're wearing high-tops? In the jungle?"

"They're actually not that—"

"We can talk about it later. We have to move. And don't look so sad and disappointed, you three. Of course I'm happy to see you. All five of you. But there are dangerous men in the area."

"We know," Ava said.

"Jack kind of bumped into them," Pepedro added.

"What?"

I pointed back toward the waterfall. "They're over that way, and any minute now they're probably going to come looking for us."

Hank glared at the two Brazilians. "Why would you bring them here? How did you even find me?"

"This wasn't our idea," Alicia answered. She pointed to Ava. "She found you. Not us."

"But how did you—" A tree branch cracked in the distance. Hank stared into the jungle, standing perfectly still. Then he breathed. "This isn't the time for questions. We need to get somewhere safe. Follow me. I have a campsite nearby."

As Hank slipped away into the jungle, I couldn't stifle my excitement. His hideout probably wouldn't have couches. Or a gaming console. But an air mattress? That was a possibility. And a nice roof was pretty much guaranteed. Maybe even a way to make coffee. Oh, he had probably come up with a way to dry socks, too. We marched ahead in silence, and my visions of Hank's secret jungle hideaway blurred and faded. All I could think about was the pain. My feet were swollen and sore. The skin between my toes had been rubbed raw. My arm ached. And even though I brushed my teeth two or even three times a day, it felt like tiny little hairs were growing on my tongue.

At one point, I reached ahead for something to hold and a thorn pressed into the base of my thumb. Yet I was so tired and busted that I barely noticed. I dropped to the back of our group. My siblings weren't doing much better. Ava's neck was covered in reddish welts. Matt couldn't stop itching his head, and he was convinced some mutant strain of lice had started a new colony in his curls.

Now that we were deep into the jungle, we didn't need to hack our way forward. Very little sunlight leaked through the thick canopy, so not many plants and bushes were growing near the muddy ground. A flock of birds started screeching and hollering as we climbed a steep hill. I fell to my knees, too tired to even try to balance. Ahead of me, Ava was grabbing roots to pull herself along. I followed behind her. My hands ached. My fingers were cramping. My toes felt like they were on fire. But I reminded myself that we were going to be at Hank's hideout soon. We were going to be safe. Maybe even comfortable. I would have dry socks.

Then the famous inventor stopped at the top of the hill and stood proudly in the center of a clearing no bigger than the kitchen in our apartment back home. "Welcome!"

At first, the area looked no different than the rest of the jungle. Then Hank began pointing things out. A waterproof bag was stuffed into one bush. A metal cooking stove with a small propane tank was tucked into the leaves beneath it. A few small pans and utensils were hidden away, as well. Hank walked around a tree and retrieved a chair built out of roughly cut branches and limbs. The cushioned seat was made of a tightly packed pile of leaves held in place with some kind of vine. He caught us all eyeing his creation. "Sorry, there's only one," he said.

"Wait, is this your campsite?"

Hank stood and held his arms wide. "Luxurious, right? It has all you'd ever need. Obviously I keep all the necessities stashed away in case any unwanted visitors hike through."

"Do you have Wi-Fi?" I asked.

"Well, no, not Wi-Fi . . ."

"We're in the jungle, Jack," Matt reminded me.

There was no roof. No mattress. He probably didn't have a way to dry my socks, either. I wanted to cry. But Hank laughed and charged at me with a smile. No one-armed guy hug this time, either. He fully embraced each of us, including Pepedro and Alicia, and although I'm not keeping score, I kind of think my hug was a little longer.

Exhausted, we swung our backpacks off our shoulders. I started to set mine on the ground when Hank grabbed it.

175

He looped a rope through one of the straps, then fed that end through everyone else's packs. Quickly, he tied a draw hitch, which is kind of like a bow-tie knot but with only one loop. Pepedro nodded in appreciation. Then Hank handed the boy with the million dollar foot the other end of the rope. He climbed up a nearby tree, swung the rope over a thick limb, and pulled it down. Pepedro passed the end to Matt, who yanked on it, hand over hand, until he lifted the bags from the forest floor. When the bags were ten feet from the ground, Hank told him to stop and tied the loose end off on a low branch.

"That's perfect," he said. "Too high for the ground dwellers, too low for our friends in the trees."

The inventor flopped back down into his seat. Then he reached behind him, under his rain jacket, and adjusted his belt. No, not his belt. Matt elbowed me and pointed.

"Why are you all staring at my fanny pack?" Hank asked. "And please, please explain to me why you tracked me all the way into the depths of the Amazon rainforest when, as you can see, I'm perfectly capable of taking care of myself."

And so we talked, and Hank listened. For a while he just sat there with his legs crossed, leaning his chin on his closed right fist. By the time we'd reached the Bobby part of the story, he jumped up and started pacing around the small clearing. "And the lab? Did you have someone take care of things before you left?"

I glanced at Matt. We were stuck in the middle of the jungle, hiding from a couple of dudes with a gun, and Hank was worried about the lab? Seriously?

"We drained the tank," Ava said, "and Min said she'd bring in a crew to finish the cleanup. She said she knew a guy."

Hank grunted. "A guy? Okay. Well, now, about this Bobby person. Did he give you a last name?"

"No," I answered.

"Could you describe him again?"

Alicia stood at the edge of the small clearing and stared out at the jungle. "Are you sure we're safe here?" she asked.

"Very," Hank said. "I purposely situated myself here because a flock of macaws nest nearby at the base of the hill. You heard them on the way up, right? If anyone comes close, they screech." He squinted at the trees in the distance. "You know, now that I think about it, they tend to squawk at just about anything, so maybe it's not a perfect alarm. But let's get back to this Bobby person. I don't remember meeting him."

"Then how would he even know about the battery idea?" Ava asked. "Did you tell anyone else what you were doing?"

First Hank shook his head. Then he stared up at the canopy and tapped his chin. "Well, there was this one time . . . I kind of got excited about the eels. Several months ago, I was at a private conference in Aspen. There were only a few hundred people—"

"A few hundred people?" Ava asked.

"Yes, well, I assumed it was a safe crowd. Mostly technology leaders, billionaires, a few government representatives, and innovators like myself. They even had a magician." For some reason he looked at me. "Normally I don't go in for that sort of thing, Jack, but he did the most fascinating card tricks. There was this one—"

"Hank," I said, louder than normal. "The conference. What did you tell them about the eels?"

"I discussed all the potential applications—the battery, the Taser, energy storage—in great detail."

"And you're surprised your secret got out?" Alicia asked.

"Yes! Typically, it's all very confidential at the Aspen conference. One of the billionaires walks around the whole time wearing a mask and headpiece that makes him look like a minotaur, and nobody says a word. Nothing leaves Aspen."

"Or so you thought," Ava pointed out.

"Right. The moment I returned to the lab, I had this feeling I was being watched. Then I actually did notice people watching me." Hank thought quietly. "This Bobby fellow. I wonder. What if he was at the conference? Someone did call me several times and offer to buy the designs to the battery. Many times. He was quite a nuisance."

"You said no?" I asked.

"Adamantly."

"How much did he offer?" I asked.

"So he decided to steal the designs instead, right?" Alicia said.

"Yes, I suppose so."

"Hank," Ava started. "We've been wondering—"

"Do you have this drive he's looking for?" Alicia asked, cutting her off.

With a smile, Hank tapped his fanny pack. "Of course," he said. "Safe and sound." He turned to Ava and Matt. "You know, I sometimes wonder if the drive itself is more innovative than the ideas it stores. It's impossible to copy. Very secure. And when I'm not carrying it around in the middle of the jungle, I can track its location to a fraction of a meter."

My sister was still trying to squeeze in her question, but Pepedro jumped in. "Why do you need to track it? In case someone steals it?"

"Yes, that's definitely an application," Hank answered. "But I actually designed that feature in case I lost the drive in the lab. I'm always misplacing things. Which reminds me,

Matt, Ava, Jack, did any of you see my favorite earphones lying around the lab? The red ones? I thought I'd packed them for this trip but—"

"Stop," Ava said, her voice forceful. "Please," she added. "We can talk about your earphones later. I'm trying to ask you a question. We told you why we came looking for you. But you still haven't explained what you're doing here."

"Yes, of course. I came for the eels, as I'm sure they told you, and we have so, so much to talk about on that front, but I returned to the Amazon for very different reasons. I assume, since you're here, that you found the map online?"

I elbowed Ava. "She did."

"By the way, how are you connecting with the satellite?" Matt asked.

Hank reached around the back of a small tree and retrieved a bow. Then he struck the pose of an archer and fired an imaginary arrow into the canopy. "An ancient idea, updated," he said. "Arrows with radio transmitters wired into the shaft. You fire them up into the canopy, and they can communicate with the satellite."

He tossed the bow to Matt. My brother dropped it.

"Min said you had taken up archery," I recalled.

Hank stood up straighter. "You spoke to Min? Does she know you're here? I imagine she's annoyed with me for—"

"To be honest, we're all kind of annoyed," Matt said.

I hadn't expected him to be the one to say it.

Hank turned quiet. My sister steered the conversation back to technology. "So at every one of those red dots on the map, an arrow is up in the canopy somewhere, sending a signal?" she asked.

"Exactly," Hank said. "What do you think is special about those locations?"

I raised my hand. What? It's a habit. And Hank pointed to me. "Eels?"

"Yes!" Hank said. "But no. Or that's not the reason I highlighted the area, anyway."

"Are those the spots where the loggers are planning to chop down trees?" Pepedro asked.

"Precisely!" Hank said. He addressed my siblings. "After my first trip with Alicia and Pepedro here, I discovered what these wood poachers were planning, but the authorities, the government, even the environmental groups—they all told me they were powerless. No trees had been cut down. I still don't know who these loggers are working for. And even if I did know, the authorities couldn't accuse someone of a crime they hadn't committed yet."

"Why not?" Alicia asked.

"That wouldn't be fair. Jack, it would be the equivalent of me withholding your allowance to punish you for the next prank e-mail you send from my account."

"I haven't sent one since—"

"Yet we both know you will."

That was true. "Okay . . ."

"Still, I can't punish you, right?"

"Right," Alicia answered. "Go on."

"Wait," I interrupted. "So am I in trouble or not?"

"No, not yet," Hank continued. "Neither are these loggers—not yet. Not until they commit a crime. I've been following these men for weeks, tracking them and their activities. When my satellite flies overhead, it picks up the transmissions from my arrows, then takes pictures of those specific locations every time it returns. Then, once we see proof of illegal logging, we can send the photos to the government, the rainforest protection groups—anyone who'll listen, really."

Ava circled the small camp. "That way, once they start cutting down the trees, all those groups will find out immediately."

"And then the authorities can stop them before they do too much damage," Matt added.

"Exactly," Hank said.

"Cool," Ava said. "But wait . . . you have the arrows, but how do the loggers keep track of these spots they want to cut down?"

"For a while they tried to use transmitters, too, but their system had a weakness no one would have considered."

"What was wrong with it?" Matt asked.

"Electrophorus electricus magnus!" Hank declared.

Pepedro responded in Portuguese. It sounded like the Brazilian version of "Huh?"

"The giant electric eel," Matt explained. "But how . . ."

Birds started squawking in the distance. I tensed. "Hank, is that your security—"

"No, that's just chatter," he said, then focused on my brother. "The loggers would place the transmitters high up on the trees, but not high enough. When these eels strike their prey, they generate an electric field so strong that it confuses their transmitters, scrambling their signals."

Pepedro and Alicia were staring out at the jungle. The birds were quiet again. Pepedro turned back to me and shrugged. Hank was right; the creatures yelled at everything, anyway. Maybe they'd just gotten annoyed with some howler monkeys. I refocused on the geniuses, and Hank was still talking about electric fields. I knew this was a science concept. One that Matt had mastered at age ten, probably. But I couldn't help imagining a field full of people playing soccer, getting jolted by little blasts of electricity every so often. That would be an amazing sport. You could just picture some guy juking a bunch of players, finding an open lane to the goal, lining up his shot . . . and then getting shocked three feet off the turf. The only way to improve it would be to add river otters.

183

Maybe they could be the goalies.

"Jack, why are you smiling?"

"What? Oh, nothing. Go on."

"So I was saying, the eels effectively kept their system from working," Hank said.

"It's almost like the creatures were protecting the jungle," Alicia added.

"Yes, well, it didn't stop the loggers. They just resorted to old-fashioned maps to track the locations."

Matt backhanded me in the shoulder. I'd completely forgotten about the map. I pulled it out and handed it to Hank. "Like this one?" I asked.

Hank pointed to the logo in the upper right corner. Then he showed it to Alicia and Pepedro. "Do you know this company?"

"It's called 'Super Floor,'" I said.

Hank clapped. "Finally! Now we actually know who's behind all this. Great work, all of you."

"Do you know when they plan to start cutting down the trees?"

Before Hank could answer, Pepedro spun around and stared over my shoulder. His expression frightened me. My heart started pounding. Three heavy steps followed, and then a hand covered with wiry black hairs gripped my shoulder. I turned.

184

Roger's steaming breath smelled like cigars. Alex ripped the map from Hank's hands. Roger grabbed the bow from Matt, leaned one end into the mud, and stepped hard on the center, snapping it in half.

"Now that we know how to stop your friend," Alex said, "we can begin clearing this area very soon."

185

13
AN UNEXPECTED RETURN

SURE, THERE WERE SIX OF US AND TWO OF THEM. BUT three geniuses, a miniature soccer star, his teenaged sister, and a handsome but skinny thirteen-year-old with a fondness for bow ties weren't about to fight a pair of Brazilian loggers. In case any one of us was considering that option, though, Roger pulled his jacket aside to reveal the gun holstered at his hip. Hank tried to reason with them, and Alicia argued with the pair in Portuguese, but they told us to be quiet. Actually, ordered would be more accurate. They made us leave our gear and then marched us back the way we'd come.

"The birds warned us," Alicia whispered. "We should have known."

Hank shrugged. "I assumed that was a false positive."

Alicia looked back to me for an explanation, but Alex silenced us. "I said quiet!" he growled.

We turned left around the wide base of a tree, moving off the trail we'd followed with Hank. The ground sloped down, then stretched out into a flat, soaked section of the forest scattered with enormous trees that looked like wooden columns in a giant, dark basement. Thin shafts of light filtered through the occasional breaks in the leafy roof. Green shoots stood up out of a dark pond. The water swirled briefly, then became still again. Roger was checking the map, leading the way. Ahead of me, Matt paused as Pepedro pointed to the canopy. A roaring, almost whining noise in the distance was growing louder fast.

"Is that a helicopter?" Matt said.

"Yes," Alex said, "our friends are here."

Roger folded the map. The canopy was too thick to see clearly, but the helicopter's spinning blades pushed aside the leaves enough for us to catch a glimpse of two men leaning out on opposite landing skids. As the helicopter hovered, they leaped off, but they didn't fall. Instead, they lowered gradually down through the tangled branches, each man hanging by a gleaming cable. One of them was small and thin, with curly bleached hair and a high forehead. He was maybe a decade older than Matt, and he smiled down at us, revealing a set of bright white teeth that belonged in a horse's mouth. We recognized the other man immediately, and not just because he was still wearing purple lacrosse shorts. My piranha-catching fishing buddy was waving as he dropped to the jungle floor. He

187

unhooked himself from the steel cable and stomped across the muddy ground.

Ava groaned. "Seriously?"

Matt scratched his head. "You called a helicopter?"

"You know this man?" Hank asked.

Bobby was grinning as he held out his hand. "You should know me, too, Dr. Witherspoon. It's an honor to meet you again," he said. "I heard you speak in Aspen." He smirked at each of us. "Resourceful bunch of kids you've got here, Hank. What gave me away, Jack?"

"You knew we were from Brooklyn," I said, "and you never asked our names."

"Plus you were a really terrible captain and your accent wasn't close to believable," Ava added. "How did you even get that boat?"

Bobby tilted his head toward his fellow helicopter passenger. "So many details, so little time. First let me introduce you to my friend Joao here."

The man with the bleached hair bowed, then shook hands with Roger and Alex, speaking quietly in Portuguese. He was as fit as a soccer player, and his eyebrows were way too perfect. I'm pretty sure he put gel in them.

"Obviously I was hoping you'd lead me straight to Hank," Bobby continued. "But I managed to radio Joao. Luckily enough, he was already scheduled to come pick up

Roger and Alex, so he grabbed me along the way." Bobby shrugged and smirked again. "Now look at us. You may have ditched me briefly—twice, if you count that chauffeur I hired to drive you around—but you led me right to him."

His words were like a punch to the stomach. I couldn't even look at Hank. We'd flown down here to help him. And we'd ruined everything.

"What do you want?" Hank asked.

"Oh, I think you know," Bobby answered. "If you'd just sold me your idea, we wouldn't be having any of this trouble."

Joao patted Roger on the shoulder. Then he shooed me out of the way and swept his hand across the top of a log, clearing some wet leaves. He sat down on his makeshift bench, unzipped his backpack, and removed a slim laptop. "Okay," he said. "I'm ready."

"Ready for what?" Alicia asked.

"Ready for the drive," Joao said.

Bobby held out his hand. "You can hand it over nicely, Hank, or one of these men can take it from you."

"Nicely is fine," Hank said. He moved the fanny pack around to the front of his waist and began poking through the contents.

"Don't give it to them," Ava urged.

Alicia stood in front of Hank. "We'll make a deal—"

189

"No deals," Bobby snapped. "He missed that chance."

The inventor was already holding out the drive, a square metallic device about the size of a stick of underarm deodorant. Bobby grabbed it out of his hands. "This is it?"

"You flip open the lid," Hank explained, "and then hold that to the side of the laptop. It attaches magnetically."

"Clever," Bobby said.

Eyebrows raised, he opened the lid and handed the device to Joao. Our newest visitor inspected it briefly, then reached out and jabbed it against the side of Bobby's leg. Instantly, my fishing buddy jumped and shook like an electrified cartoon character. He started hopping around, shaking his arms, crying in pain.

190

Calmly, Joao turned to Hank. "A Taser? Very clever. This would have wiped out my computer, yes?"

Hank shrugged. "Maybe?"

Alex reached out and grabbed the fanny pack from Hank, then passed it to Joao. "Next time," Joao said, "I will use it on one of the children. Or you can tell me which of these little things"—he held out the open fanny pack—"is the drive."

Hank pointed to a device slightly larger than my thumb. Carefully, Joao removed a cap and revealed a metallic square designed to plug into a computer. Joao said something in Portuguese and inserted the drive into the computer.

Still shaken, Bobby clenched his fists and breathed in deeply. Veins in his neck were bulging as he moved toward us.

Matt, Ava, and I all stepped back.

"Be calm, Bobby, be calm," Joao said without looking up. "It was just a little shock."

"Look for the battery designs first," Bobby mumbled.

"There's something you should know about the battery," Hank began.

"Yeah, that it's mine now," Bobby said. He turned to Joao. "That's our deal, right?"

The bluish light of the computer screen glowed on Joao's face. "Sure, sure," he muttered. "The battery is yours."

"Wait," Ava said, "then why do you want the drive?"

Joao lifted his hand and traced a circle in the air. "The trees," he said. He squinted up toward the canopy, then pointed. "As I understand it, this drive allows me to control your satellite, too. Is that right, Hank?"

"No?"

I shook my head. Hank was a terrible liar, and Joao didn't believe him for a second. "We can't have you taking pictures of our work and preventing us from removing these beautiful trees," Joao said. "The password, please."

Ava tugged at Hank's shirt. "Don't give it to him."

"Don't listen to her," Joao said. "It's just a few trees. There are more important things to worry about."

"These are not just trees!" Alicia shouted. "They're a precious resource."

"Give me the password and we can all go on with our lives."

"And I'll get my battery design," Bobby added.

Joao flicked his fingers toward Bobby without looking. "Yes, yes, you'll get your battery. I already told you that."

"And if we don't help you?" I asked.

The bleached-blond crook scowled. "There's a small river near here. Roger and Alex here will make you swim with the piranhas until you talk."

"Don't do it, Hank," Ava said. "We can't let them win."

"But I can't let them hurt you," Hank said. "This isn't about winning or losing. It's about not getting ourselves killed."

Then he mumbled a phrase.

My sister swung toward him. "Are you serious? That's your password? 'Science rules'? I told you about password security, Hank! It can't be that simple."

"It's all capital letters," Hank added with a shrug. "And there's an exclamation point at the end."

"Plus, it's true," Matt said. Pepedro and Alicia stared at him. "What? Science does rule."

Hank grinned.

Did they have to be nerds at a moment like this? Yes. The answer was always yes.

Without looking up, Joao said, "I'm in." He squinted, clicked, ran his index finger along the screen. "This is it. This is definitely it. The designs are all here, too. Some very interesting stuff," he added, looking up at Hank.

"What about the battery?" Bobby asked.

"Be patient," Joao replied. He held up one index finger and traced the other along the screen. He clicked and scrolled, then nodded, like he was following a drumbeat only he could hear. "You see," Joao continued, "my boss cannot have people believing that we are cutting down the jungle. That would be terrible for business."

"But . . . that's exactly what you're doing," Ava said.

"This is what you say," Joao replied. "But without the satellite pictures, you have no proof."

"Who is your boss, anyway?" I asked.

Joao ignored me. He hit a button on his keypad, then sat back and crossed his arms. "Now that I control the satellite, there will be no pictures, and without the proof, there is no crime." He smiled wide and closed his laptop. "In two days, the skies will be swarming with helicopters plucking trees from the forest, and we will all make so, so much money."

"You are traitors to your land," Alicia said.

193

"To the planet," Hank added.

"You're criminals!" Pepedro shouted.

"Perhaps," Joao said. "But rich ones!"

Bobby pointed to the laptop. "Wait, can you turn that on again and show me the battery design?"

"And may I have my fanny pack back?" Hank asked.

Joao moved the contents of the pack around with his finger, then zipped it up and tossed it to Hank. "Why not?" he said.

Bobby reached for the laptop. "The battery. Can I just—"

"Patience!" Joao shouted. "I told you. Please."

"I'm tired of waiting," Bobby said. "Let me see the design. We have a deal."

Roger and Alex stepped between Joao and Bobby.

The helicopter was approaching.

"Unfortunately, my friend, our deal has changed," Joao said. "My boss would like these batteries, too. We will keep the design ourselves."

The two loggers blocked Bobby as he lunged for Joao's computer. He stopped, then shifted one foot in front of the other and rolled his head around his shoulders, cracking his neck. "That's not going to happen. I'm a black belt in several different styles of martial arts and I—"

Unfortunately, Bobby never finished his sentence.

194

Roger's right fist flashed forward as quickly as a golden lancehead and smashed into Bobby's forehead.

He dropped like a puppet without strings.

Joao winced. "I thought he would block it."

Alex laughed, then called to Roger in Portuguese. He walked over to Bobby and began untying his boots.

"You're taking his shoes?" Matt asked.

"We're taking all your shoes," Roger replied. "Don't worry. These two are good guides. You'll survive. But this will slow you down long enough for us to finish our work here in the jungle."

"You're not serious?" I asked.

Roger tapped Alex, who showed us the pistol once more.

Okay, so they were serious.

Alex stared at my sneakers. "Why are you wearing basketball shoes in the jungle?"

I untied them. Hank, the geniuses, and Alicia did the same. Pepedro started to unlace his boots when Joao stopped him. "No, no, that left foot, we must protect. You can keep yours."

Ava protested. "Are you kidding me? That's not fair!"

"You aren't the future of Brazilian football," Joao said.

The noise from the helicopter's engines grew from a distant whir to a rhythmic roar as we tossed our shoes into a pile. Three steel cables with large harnesses dropped through the canopy. Joao stepped into his harness first; then Alex and Roger followed, each of them holding two or three pairs of shoes. Taunting Hank, Joao held his hands together in a false sign of gratitude. "Thank you," he mouthed.

Alex yelled into his handheld radio. The harnesses rose, and Joao waved good-bye, leaving us mostly shoeless and completely stranded in the middle of the rainforest.

14
CHERYL TO THE RESCUE

SO THIS IS WEIRD. I KNOW. BUT DURING THE WALK BACK TO Hank's camp, I started thinking how it would have been nice if Min showed up. Back home, she had some kind of internal sensor that told her when we really needed her. Sometimes she'd just pop into the apartment to say hello at the exact moment my thoughts started spinning in some dark direction. Or she'd show up with soup when one of us was feeling sick. The jungle was hot, and I wasn't all that hungry, and I know this doesn't make sense, but as we trudged ahead, I wanted Min to bring me soup.

Mud was seeping up between my toes with each step. Treading on the slightest root or twig sent a jolt of pain up through my foot. But Matt wasn't complaining, and Ava was marching ahead without making a sound, so I kept my mouth shut, too. Pepedro kept offering his boots to Ava and me, but she didn't accept them, so neither could I.

We also had another member of our group now.

Although part of me wanted to leave him, Bobby dragged along behind us, cursing and swearing to himself as he struggled to keep pace. Meanwhile, Hank was annoyingly cheerful. Maybe it was the fact that he'd been alone in the jungle for three weeks and finally had some company. Or maybe, as he claimed, he really did like the feel of the raw ground on his feet. Either way, I couldn't see any reason for us to be happy. Not only we were stuck, but we'd completely failed. Hank's plan was ruined. The rainforest was doomed. And someone else was going to get rich off his battery designs.

Back at the campsite, Matt untied the rope and lowered our backpacks, and Hank started pulling his cookware out of the bushes. "I've been saving this," he said, holding up a foil packet. "Dehydrated French onion soup. Your favorite, right, Jack?"

No, it was Matt's favorite. And this wasn't quite what I'd been hoping for earlier. Min wasn't here. But still. He'd saved us soup. I smiled and thanked him.

"We need to find a way out of here," Ava said.

"First, we need some nourishment," Hank said. "Then we can find a solution to our current predicament."

"This isn't a predicament," Ava said. "It's a disaster."

"I agree with her," Alicia replied.

Matt found a few fallen logs and pulled them into the

clearing to use as benches. Pepedro disappeared into the jungle in search of plants and herbs to improve the soup. Bobby sat on one of the logs with his knees pulled up to his chest and a fierce scowl stretched across his face.

Alicia assured us that she and her brother would be able to get us back to the city alive. "Maybe a few scratches, some bruises, a broken bone or two in the worst case," she added. "But we'll survive. No problem. Our main concern should be stopping these criminals."

"Could we set traps or something?" Matt suggested.

"Impossible," Hank said. "You heard Joao. In a few days this place is going to be swarming with logging crews. There's no way we can stop them on the ground."

"You couldn't even stop three," Bobby mumbled.

"You weren't much help," Alicia snapped.

"Please, let's not fight," Hank said. "If we're going to figure this out, we have to be on the same team. I despise sports metaphors, but in this case, I suppose it's necessary. Bobby, are you on our team?"

"I was a swimmer and a golfer," he said. "I competed for myself. No teams."

Hank exhaled heavily. "Okay, let's try this again. Do you want to stop them from destroying the rainforest?"

"To be honest, I don't really care about the jungle." He pulled up his sleeve and ran his hand over a bunch of red welts. "And the jungle definitely doesn't care about us. But yes, I want to stop them. They stole my battery designs."

"My designs," Hank corrected him. "But still, we can work with that. Let's discuss our options."

As Hank prepared the soup and Pepedro added in handfuls of herbs, we talked through a few different ways we might prevent the crews from cutting down the trees. Unfortunately, all of them pretty much stunk. When the broth was ready, we brought out our folding plastic bowls; Bobby didn't have one, but Hank tossed him his and said he'd eat from the pot. Hank served the soup, and for a few minutes we sipped in silence. Matt was slurping up his broth, and Hank winced, but he didn't say anything.

Surprisingly, in all the plans that the geniuses, Alicia, and Bobby suggested, none of them had mentioned my siblings' satellite. "What about Cheryl?" I asked.

"Who's Cheryl?" Hank asked.

I explained.

A fine mist of soup sprayed out of Hank's mouth. "Wait. What? You two launched a CubeSat?"

Matt blushed.

"You were the one who suggested it," Ava reminded Hank. "After we got back from Hawaii. Remember?"

"Vaguely. But you actually built it? That's amazing! How did you get it—I mean, Cheryl—into orbit?"

"Well, you had already secured two spots on the rocket, and when your backup CubeSat failed, Jack e-mailed a few people and we sent ours to the launch company instead."

Hank glared at me. I shrugged. "What?"

"Okay," he continued, nodding. "Understood. And really," he said, focusing on the geniuses again, "I'm amazed. Astounded!"

"Totally," I cut in, "and they can tell you all about how they built it later." I pointed at my siblings. "If you can connect to your satellite, can't you just get it to take photos of the area? Can't you program it to do what Hank's satellite was supposed to do?"

"You can't program anything without a computer," Bobby said. His know-it-all tone was cosmically annoying.

"Matt has his laptop," I noted.

"We don't exactly have Wi-Fi around here," Matt said. "We'd need a big antenna if we want to connect to the satellite."

The three geniuses were silent. Normally, I would've been worried. But this was a very particular type of silence. Their faces were blank and their brains were so busy that their bodies looked paralyzed.

My brother squinted at Ava, who turned to Hank. He shrugged back at her. "The arrow could be the antenna."

"We could write the code to reprogram Cheryl."

"Then if we connect the laptop to the antenna—"

"Does the laptop have a name?" Pepedro interrupted.

"She names things, not him," I explained.

"We'll call it Ronaldo," Pepedro said.

Alicia leaned toward me. "He was a great footballer."

"Okay," Matt said, "so we connect Ronaldo to the arrow—"

"Pete," Hank suggested. "I had a childhood friend named Pete. He was very resourceful. Ronaldo connects to Pete, then Pete talks to Cheryl."

"And Cheryl takes the pictures," Ava finished.

Matt was biting his lower lip. "We still have to get Pete up into the trees, so there's a clear line of sight to Cheryl."

"I brought Betsy," Ava reminded him.

"Who is Betsy?" Alicia asked. "A friend of Cheryl?"

The geniuses didn't even hear her question. "We need someone to use Betsy to get up there," Matt said.

"Up where?" Alicia asked.

"The roof of the rainforest," Hank said.

"Stop," Pepedro said. "Can you please explain to us what you're talking about?"

Hank grabbed a stick off the ground, then kneeled in the dirt and began to draw in the center of the clearing. He started with a long, curved line. "This is Earth, okay?" Next he drew a squiggly semicircle on the planet's surface and a small "x" inside. "This is the rainforest, and this is us, on the floor."

Bobby scooted forward. "Where am I?"

Hank thought he was joking. I leaned forward and pointed to a random spot in the center of the jungle. "You're there," I said.

"Good," Bobby said. "Go on, Dr. Witherspoon."

Our mentor was staring at Bobby as though he'd just spoken in Klingon. Hank breathed in through his teeth, then continued, drawing a small square high above the roof of the rainforest, with an arrow showing its path above the surface. "When you launch a satellite into space, it completes a circuit of the planet every ninety minutes or so."

"So it passes over our heads once every ninety minutes?" I asked.

"That's fast," Bobby commented.

"Yes," Hank said, "it is fast, but no, it doesn't exactly pass over our heads every ninety minutes."

Matt was nodding along. "It takes at least a few days for a satellite in one of these orbits to return to the same spot overhead, because the Earth's spin is not the same as the satellite's speed, and Cheryl's orbit is a little tilted."

Alicia pointed up. "So when exactly is Cheryl coming back?"

Neither Matt nor Ava had an answer. "That's a really

203

good question," my brother replied. He removed his laptop and started typing. "I can't get online, obviously, but I should be able to look at our old data of the satellite's path and figure out when it's going to cruise overhead again."

"Yeah," Bobby said, "you do that."

Ava was pacing. "If we can connect with Cheryl, we could also have Internet access."

"Can I check YouTube?" The question shot out of my mouth like a rocket. The guy in the overalls was definitely sleeping. And Ava was glaring at me. "What? I'm joking!"

"No, you're not checking anything," Ava said. "But we could start alerting people."

"I have all the right contacts in the government and rainforest organizations," Hank said. "I could draft e-mails warning them about the planned activities."

"Then if we program Cheryl to take pictures and post them online," Ava continued, "they'll be able to see proof of what's happening."

"And then the government will be able to stop them," Alicia said. "This makes sense. This could actually work."

"Some of the trees will fall," Ava noted.

"But we could save so many more," Pepedro added.

Matt whistled. "I have good news and bad news," he said. "Cheryl is set to fly overhead on Saturday afternoon, the day the logging starts."

"That makes today Thursday?" Hank asked. "I honestly have no idea. I lost track of the days a while ago."

"Yes," Alicia replied. "Today is Thursday, and we should be able to catch them before they do too much damage."

I watched my brother. "What's the bad news?" I asked.

"Well, we have to reprogram her before that if we want to alert everyone."

"And . . ."

"And the only other time she's going to be overhead before that is in"—he clicked a few buttons on his keyboard—"roughly four hours. At a little after one o'clock this afternoon."

"So we need to get that computer up in the canopy in less than four hours?" I asked.

"Right."

Hank clapped and started wringing his hands together. "Okay, then. Let's get to work!"

Ava held up her climbing device. "I'll make sure Betsy is ready."

"I'll start working on the code to reprogram the satellite," my brother added.

"I'll focus on the antenna," Hank said.

"Maybe Pepedro and I can find a good tall tree?" Alicia suggested.

"That would be fantastic," Hank said. "Ideally one that rises above the canopy."

"What should I do?" Bobby asked.

"Why don't you look for a possible tree, too?" Hank suggested. "Alicia, you two head south. Bobby, you look to the north."

My fishing buddy clapped his hands. "Got it," he said. "Which way is north?"

Hank pointed, and Bobby was on his way.

So now Alicia and Pepedro had a task. The geniuses were busy. Bobby had a job, too: to get out of the way. I wasn't going to be able to tune up Betsy. I wasn't capable of reprogramming Cheryl or fixing up Pete. But I had to help somehow. I gazed up at the canopy. "So how far up am I going, anyway?"

Everyone stopped what they were doing and stared at me.

Hank spoke first. "You don't have to—"

"I'm too heavy," Matt said. Then, with his eyebrows raised, he added, "Isn't that right, Ava?"

"Someone your size might burn out the battery too quickly," she said. "You, too, Hank."

"It's fine," I said. "I'm going."

Alicia laid her hand on my shoulder. "They said you were very brave."

They did? That was nice of them. Definitely. But sometimes I wasn't so sure. There's a very thin line between brave and stupid, and I dance around it way too often.

15
THE SLOTH LORD

WE FINISHED OUR PREPARATIONS A FEW MINUTES before noon. Alicia lent me her wristwatch to track the time. The geniuses had readied a backpack for me with all the key equipment, including the laptop, and we started down the path. Bobby was mad that Hank had chosen Alicia and Pepedro's kapoktree, not the one he'd picked out, and he spent most of the walk talking about his father, the owner of the second largest car dealership in New England. His dad wanted him to move into the car business, too, but Bobby refused. Instead, he had tried to start a bunch of his own companies, including Kwik Kale, a chain of vegan fast-food restaurants, and Male Salon, a nail spa that served only men. All of them had failed.

At some point, I stopped listening and started thinking about the task ahead of me. My hands were shaking already. If I was going to climb up into the canopy, I needed inspiration. I needed to connect with this rainforest on a deeper level. I needed to be one with the jungle. I interrupted Bobby and asked, "How do you say sloth in Portuguese?"

"Preguiça," Alicia answered, drawing out the last two syllables so they sounded like geese-ah.

"Why?" Pepedro asked.

"No reason," I lied.

The sloth might not have seemed like the most inspiring choice. I was going to need to move quickly. Plus I definitely got the chills whenever I imagined all those beetles living in its fur. And I was way more regular than once a week. So we weren't exactly alike. But the sloth was my spirit animal. I was no longer Jack. I was Preguiça.

Matt reminded me that our one opportunity to connect with Cheryl before Saturday was only an hour away. If we missed that, we'd have to wait another week, and that would be too late. He didn't need to tell me twice. But he did, anyway.

Once we talked through all the details, we reviewed them again. And again. After what felt like the fiftieth time, I said, "I'm starting to think you guys don't trust me."

No one answered. At least they didn't lie.

My feet were aching, but Matt's were worse. He must have stubbed his toes twenty times on the walk. When we arrived at the base of the enormous tree, I stared up into the green shadows of the canopy. Was I really going up there?

I noticed that Hank was watching me. One corner of his mouth was angling upward slightly. I considered going in for a hug, even the one-armed guy version. Instead I just nodded. My sister was straight-faced and serious. She quietly wished me luck. Matt offered a fist bump. Then he winked. "You can do this, Jack," he said.

But Jack was gone. I was Preguiça, Sloth Lord of the forest, and I had no time for emotions.

The tree looked impossibly tall. The base was easily ten feet wide. It flared out at the bottom and narrowed as it rose. A monkey hiding somewhere in the canopy roared down at us. Vines thicker than baseball bats hung from the branches high overhead. I grabbed one.

"I think it would be better to use Betsy," Pepedro whispered. He pointed to a thick limb in the canopy high above us. "See that one?"

I squinted. "Pretty much."

"Maybe aim for that?"

Ava helped me strap into Betsy's harness, which was kind of like a babyproof swing seat, and buckled it around my waist. The device was made up of a football-size spool of wire, a powerful electric motor, and a super awesome wrist-mounted crossbow. Following Ava's instructions, I connected the thin line from the spool to a metal dart and clipped it into the miniature crossbow. She was watching me to make sure I did it right. I pulled back the dart to load the device.

"Okay?" I asked.

"It's all you," she said.

I lifted my hand, closed one eye, aimed, and fired.

The dart shot high into the tree, trailing the thin line.

And it completely missed.

Just two attempts later—or maybe four—I had my bull's-eye. The dart dug into the limb.

"Test it," Ava suggested.

I pulled with all my might.

"Good," she said. "If it's going to come loose, you want it to come loose now, when you're on the ground, not a hundred feet off the floor."

Sometimes my sister was a little too direct.

"But it won't come loose," Hank added. "Right, Ava?"

She hesitated. "Oh, sure. Right. Of course not."

I flipped the switch that converted Betsy to climbing mode. Do I wish I'd tried the thing out beforehand? Definitely. Especially since the one time I messed around with Betsy, I almost broke my finger. And the last test I'd seen ended with Ava splashing into the dive tank in Hank's lab. But there was no time for a practice session. The motor whirred, turning the spool, and she sucked up that cable like a hungry giant slurping up the world's longest strand of spaghetti.

The line tightened.

The harness jerked around my waist.

And I flew up off the ground.

The first thirty feet were actually kind of fun, as if I'd just launched off the world's most extreme trampoline. Then I hit the lower section of the canopy. Small branches smacked me in the arms. Leaves slapped against my face. Monkeys and macaws hollered, and I jerked to a stop a forearm's length from the thick limb. I reached up, grabbed hold with two hands, and pulled myself over, into a sitting position. The dart was impossible to pull out of the tree limb, so I unclipped the wire and left the dart in the tree.

Preguiça still had two more darts remaining.

Straddling the tree limb was like sitting on the back of a giant horse. Carefully, I slid backward toward the trunk, reminding myself not to look down.

Then I looked down.

The ground was really, really far away.

Another monkey roared at me. This one was only ten feet away. Opening its huge mouth, it flashed a nasty set of teeth. Normally, I don't talk to myself. Or not much, anyway. But I needed a little pep talk, and the growling monkey wasn't helping. "Come on, Jack," I said aloud. "You're Preguiça the Sloth Lord. You live in trees. You sleep in trees. You can do this."

211

Sure, I was a hundred feet off the ground. But my siblings and Hank, my family: they were depending on me. In a rush, I attached another dart to the cable, raised the wrist gauntlet, and eyed my next target. This shot was trickier, since I had to fire it through a gap in the branches above me to reach the top of the kapok tree. Carefully, I squinted, aimed, and fired.

The dart shot toward the top of the kapok tree, burying itself near the trunk. The line held. I flipped the switch, and Betsy whisked me up through the canopy. The kapok trees rose higher than the rest of the rainforest. They poked up and out of their surroundings like seven-foot-tall basketball players scattered on a crowded city street. And now I felt like one of those giants, staring down at the top of the canopy.

Then my shoulder slammed into the trunk.

The dart was buried in the wood. I kept the line clipped in place and switched the device over to safety mode. This way, Ava had explained, the line would spool out enough for me to climb, but if I fell, Betsy would lock and keep me from dropping straight to the ground.

The trunk of the enormous tree didn't stop, exactly, but it split into five limbs at the top, almost like someone reaching their arm high into the sky with their fingers outstretched. I settled into a spot between the limbs, leaning back against one, with my feet jammed up against two others. The bark below me was decaying. I pressed into it with the heel of my hand. The wood was soft, but the surrounding trunk was still solid. Most of the kapok tree's leaves had fallen, so the view was clear, and I looked out at the surrounding jungle. The clouds had drifted away, but a layer of mist had settled on the tops of the trees below me. The thick canopy reminded me of a huge, rolling, uneven field marked by bumps and hills, carpeted with grass that had never been mowed. I checked Alicia's watch. Fifteen minutes remained until Cheryl was supposed to fly over the horizon.

But I wasn't really in a perfect position. A little higher and I'd be able to set up Pete so the antenna had a totally clear connection to the satellite. I breathed deep and climbed, pulling myself higher. The branch above me was softer than I'd expected, and wet. My fingers slid. I tried to grab on, but they slipped free, and suddenly I was grasping air. I landed barefoot on the branch below. For a second I balanced there with nothing to hold.

Then the branch cracked. My feet slid down along the length of the slick wood, and I dropped straight toward the forest floor.

16

THE ROOF OF THE

RAINFOREST

N THE LONG HISTORY OF HUMANKIND, THERE HAVE BEEN MANY great wedgies. The legendary hero Achilles gave them to his friends when they borrowed his spear. Presidents have given them to vice presidents. But when Betsy finally engaged in safety mode and stopped unwinding, the wedgie she gave me had to rank as one of the most painful. The underwear-ripping torture I'd received from the bearded twelve-year-old I briefly shared a room with when I was eight? Not even close.

Breathing slowly through my nose, I performed a systems check, like a captain at the controls of a spaceship. My brain was working. My fingers moved. My toes still burned. My feet were still aching. Sure, it felt like two construction workers had just swung a pair of sledgehammers at my butt, and we're not even going to talk about what I was feeling up front, but I'd survived. I was pretty sure I'd be able to walk. Eventually. And my backpack was still tight around my shoulders, which meant the computer and the rest of the gear was secure.

The canopy was only a few body lengths below me. My destination was now towering high above. And Betsy was beeping. "Ava!" I yelled down. "Why's this thing making noises?"

If my sister replied, I didn't hear her. The crowded canopy was like a rock concert hosted by crazed, caffeinated zoo animals. I checked Alicia's watch and panicked. Now only twelve minutes remained, and I needed to get back to the top of the tree. I clicked Betsy into climbing mode again. She was beeping slower and softer. Was that a good sign? Or a bad one?

"Don't be the battery," I muttered to myself.

Betsy pulled me upward at a painfully slow pace, and I repeated the phrase over and over, turning it into a kind of chant. But chanting wasn't going to charge a dying battery.

Ten feet from the spot where the dart was lodged into the branch, Betsy died. The motor whirred to a stop, and I was dangling with nothing to hold on to. I gripped the cable and tried to pull myself up. I was a pretty good rope climber. One time in gym class I placed seventh out of twenty kids in a contest. Or maybe it was seventeenth. Either way, this cable was far too thin to grip. I wasn't making any progress.

The trunk of the tree was only fifteen feet away, and it was scattered with the stumps of broken branches. If I got close, I could use them as steps and climb my way up.

215

Hopefully. So I swung my legs back and forth, building momentum. The clock in my head started ticking. Finally I reached out and grabbed one of the broken stumps. A splinter dug into the base of my thumb. I winced but held on and stopped swinging. Then I placed my right foot on another broken limb, found a spot for my left, and started to climb. This time I settled on a lower perch, a branch that felt far too strong to snap. The position wasn't ideal for linking up with Cheryl, but it was good enough, and I couldn't risk climbing higher. The branches up there were too weak, and I had too little time. My heart was racing again. My hands were quivering. I shifted my backpack around to the front and unzipped the main compartment. Channel Preguiça, I told myself, breathing slowly.

Find your inner sloth.

Chillax.

I checked the watch again. Seven minutes left. Setting up the antenna was my first job. Hank had modified it so that it could be connected to the computer. Now I laid it carefully along the length of the limb. Pepedro had torn some straps off his backpack so I could tie it down, and I used these to secure the half closest to me. Then, following Hank's instructions, I bent the upper portion toward the sky.

Next, I removed Matt's laptop. My hands were still shaking. I tried not to think about how much my brother loved the machine or how easily it could slip out of my grip and plummet to the ground.

Four minutes remained.

I laid the computer on top of the backpack so the front edge was pushing against my chest. A small cable extended out from the bottom of the modified arrow, and I reached around, grabbed the end, and plugged it into the computer. A light breeze drifted through the top of the trees. The branches waved and swung, opening a clear view to the sky. The spot was better than I'd guessed.

With three minutes to go, I switched on the laptop.

A million years were crammed into the next sixty seconds. The screen blinked to life. I entered Matt's password—he warned me that he'd change it the minute I got back down—and breathed a sigh of relief as the machine booted up. Luckily, Matt had made this part of the process easy. Once I launched his program, all I had to do was click the big green "connect" button in the bottom right corner of the screen. His codes would do the rest of the work.

And I tried. Honestly, I tried. But Matt's precious computer had chosen that moment to throw a mild tantrum. Alicia's watch said I had less than two minutes left. The touch screen wasn't working. I was moving my finger all around the square black pad at the base of the keys, but nothing happened. The annoying little arrow on the screen, the one

I needed to move just a few inches to the right, refused to budge. And I tried everything. Telepathy. Singing. Begging. Ava would've suggested restarting the computer. Hank probably would've told me to be patient. Pepedro? Maybe he would've kicked the machine. Lefty, of course.

Desperately, I started tapping random buttons. Nothing worked until I hit the tab key. A thin rectangle appeared around the green "connect" button. I hit enter, and Matt's laptop cooperated. "Yes!" I screamed.

Two macaws perched in another part of the tree shrieked back. Complimenting me on my stroke of genius? Maybe. Either that or they were telling me to shut up.

While the program ran in the background, I opened Hank's e-mail account and sent the messages he'd drafted.

A blue wheel appeared in the center of the screen, and a thick green bar gradually filled it in from the top, moving clockwise. First a quarter, then half. The bar was advancing slowly but steadily. The satellite's new orders were being transferred, and the machine was processing its new commands.

Cheryl was listening, and this wasn't a miracle or magic. This was pure science, the result of the very real genius of my brother and sister. Was I tempted to check YouTube to see if I'd passed sixteen million views? Of course. But I resisted. As the program and the e-mail server talked to the satellite in the background, I opened a Web browser. The laptop would only be in contact with the satellite for a few minutes at most. Then Cheryl would cruise past the horizon, and Ronaldo would be off-line.

In terms of brainpower, I can't match up with the geniuses. So any time I have a chance to do a little extra reading or research, a shot to learn something they don't already know, I take advantage. Up in the tree, I typed the name of the floor company, Super Andar, in quotes and clicked the search button. The connection was painfully slow. Only about thirty seconds remained when I clicked through to the company's site. There was nothing interesting up top. I scrolled down the page until several rows of small photographs appeared. Each picture was a portrait of one of the leaders of the company. Our bleached-blond nemesis appeared in the third row. But that wasn't the picture that surprised me. At the very top, in a row all to herself, there was a photograph of the leader of the company, the boss Joao had mentioned, and it was someone we'd already met. Someone who'd been "helping" us almost from the moment we arrived in Manaus. High above the rainforest, I stared at an image of a woman who should've had a wart on the end of her long and twisted chin.

17
DARKNESS IN THE WATER

O NCE I'D PACKED UP THE GEAR, I UNCLIPPED THE cable, wrapped it around the branch five times, and snapped it back onto the end of the dart. Betsy may have been out of battery power, but she could still unspool and lower me down. The only question was how fast I'd drop. The answer? Not quite at the speed of light, but it felt that way. Leaves and branches whipped into me as I crashed down through the canopy. Once the jungle floor was in sight, and I spotted everyone staring up at me hopefully, I realized there was one other question.

How was I going to stop?

Frantically, I started pressing buttons and flipping levers, hoping there was some juice left in the battery. Ava was shouting. The sound of the cable unspooling changed. The line ran out, and five feet from the ground, Betsy gave me my second mega-wedgie of the day.

This one might have been worse than the first.

I moaned. Matt and Hank helped me out of the harness.

Hank leaned in close, squinting as he stared into my eyes, and asked if I was injured. "No, I'll be okay," I answered.

"That was so very brave, Jack," Hank said. He shook his head. "You continue to—"

"Did it work?" Matt asked, cutting him off.

"Wait," I said. "Hank, you were saying something?"

"Never mind that," Ava said. "Did you get there in time?"

I gave them a double thumbs-up. Pepedro whooped. Hank shook his clenched fists and patted Matt on the back. Maybe I'd ask him to finish that compliment another time.

"Everything worked?" Alicia asked.

"I think so," I said. "Everything went as planned. Mostly, anyway."

"Mostly?" Hank pressed.

They didn't need to hear about my fall. "The e-mails were sent and the programs transferred," I said. "Plus I discovered something else."

When I told them Dona Maria was in charge of Super Floor, Ava and Matt were surprised. Hank was livid. The Brazilians were horrified that such an important citizen of Manaus was planning to destroy a huge section of the rainforest. And Bobby quietly traced his toe through the mud.

Alicia pointed at him. "You knew, didn't you? This whole time, you knew she was with Super Floor?"

222

Bobby shrugged.

"How could you lie to us?" Pepedro asked.

"I never lied," Bobby said. "Okay, so maybe that's not true. I definitely lied."

"A bunch of times," I added.

"Fine," Bobby admitted. "But I never lied about Dona Maria. It's just that you never asked."

"So how did you partner up with her?" Ava asked over her shoulder. "Was she the one who sent you into Hank's lab?"

"No, that was all me," Bobby said. "I staked out the neighborhood for five days before figuring out how to get inside." He glanced at Hank. "That Dumpster is a nice touch, by the way."

"So when did you meet her?" I asked.

"She contacted me after you ditched my limousine driver," Bobby explained. "Once she found out I was searching for you, Hank, she set me up with the boat, then fixed it so that I could follow the five of you straight to him. Then when you ditched me, I managed to get a message out to Joao the next day, and he picked me up in the helicopter."

"How much did she pay you?" Pepedro asked.

"She didn't need to pay me," Bobby admitted. "Our interests were aligned. We both wanted to find Dr. Witherspoon. She wanted to stop him from interfering with her logging operations, and I wanted his battery design."

223

"So did she, apparently," I added.

"Yeah, well, I hadn't counted on that," he said.

"So what now?" I asked.

Matt didn't have an answer, and neither did Ava. We all waited for Hank, and he paused for a few seconds before responding. "Now we retrieve our gear and get back to Manaus," Hank said. "We need to make sure those satellite photographs get through to the proper authorities. Plus I want my drive back."

None of us reacted. I didn't want to say it. Thankfully, Matt did first. "Hank, I'm sorry, but I don't think I can hike another three days through this jungle. Not without shoes. We need to call for help."

"We should've done it when you were up in the canopy, Jack," Ava pointed out.

"Don't worry," Hank said. "I already did. Or you did, Jack, when you sent those e-mails. The nearest river is only a few hours from here. Our ride should be there soon enough."

Slightly less than two hours later, after we grabbed all our bags from the campsite, we arrived at the edge of a small river and found the *Von Humboldt* holding its position in the center, with its bow pointing upstream.

"What's Bobby's boat doing there?" I asked.

"Bobby's boat?" Hank said. "That's my boat!"

"It is?" Matt asked.

JACK AND THE GENIUSES

"I might have lied about that, too," Bobby said.

"I designed this boat specifically for the Amazon," Hank said.

"Yes," Bobby said, "and my friends stole it."

Hank shrugged. "They did? I had no idea. I've been so busy in the jungle."

Pepedro pointed at the *Von Humboldt*. "How did she get here? We left the boat miles away."

"On the banks of a totally different river," Alicia added.

"One of those e-mails you sent a few hours ago was to the *Von Humboldt*, Jack," Hank explained. "I sent these coordinates so she'd come to pick us up. I didn't think she'd get here this quickly, though."

Matt was shaking his head. "I should have known. You named it after Alexander von Humboldt, the great scientist."

"The guy who shocked himself with electric eels," I added.

"Exactly! Impressive, Jack."

"How does it navigate?" Ava asked. "I mean, I'm guessing you have laser scanners looking for obstacles on the surface."

"And GPS when the boat is within satellite range, obviously," Matt added.

"Right, but what about the underwater hazards?" Ava pressed.

"That's where Jack helped me out."

Matt pointed at me. "Him?"

If I'd been wearing a bow tie, I would've straightened it.

"Well, not directly," Hank said. "But your suggestion about eels led me to a pretty interesting breakthrough, Jack. Electric eels don't just stun their prey with those jolts. They use an electric field to identify obstacles and fish. So I copied their technique and created a new navigation system for boats," Hank said. "The *Von Humboldt* can scan for and avoid all kinds of surface and underwater obstacles."

My siblings were mesmerized. But I'd turned my attention to another issue. At least fifty feet of open river stretched between us and the boat. That water was probably swarming with piranhas. "That's great, but how are we getting out there?" I asked.

"Oh!" Hank declared. "This part's my favorite!"

His backpack had a support belt that clipped around his waist. He reached into one of the pockets and removed a small radio with a stubby antenna. He caught Pepedro and Alicia staring. "I know what you're thinking, but it's short-range only. I couldn't have used it to call for help."

"What's it for, then?" Alicia asked.

Hank lifted his eyebrows three times, quickly. "It's a remote control," he said. As he pressed a button on the side of the radio, two panels opened on the roof of the cabin. An aluminum shaft telescoped up out of the hidden compartment and unfolded into a crane with a steel cable at the end. The crane lifted a large plastic case from the roof, swung it out over the edge of the *Von Humboldt*, and lowered it into the water below.

The case unfolded before it hit the water. A slightly larger version of our failed fishing boat quickly inflated and cruised across the water, aiming straight for Hank.

"Are you steering?" Ava asked.

"No, it tracks the radio," he explained. "It will drive straight to the remote control."

But the boat never made it to Hank. Standing knee-deep in the golden water, Bobby grabbed the bow, then swung it around and shut off the electric motor.

"What are you doing?" Hank asked.

Alicia started moving to the boat when Bobby held up his free hand. "Stop!" he said.

"Why?" Ava asked.

Slowly, Bobby was backing into deeper water.

"Bobby," Hank said, "what are you doing?"

"I'm going back to Manaus," he said, "but you're not."

"What do you mean?" Hank asked.

"What do I mean? For a genius you're not very quick, are you? I'm going to steer this little craft out to that beautiful boat of yours, return to the city, and steal the drive back from that greedy old hag."

"You're calling her greedy?" Ava snapped. "You're the thief."

Hank waded forward, holding up his hands. "Bobby, please, let's just talk this through."

Bobby backed up farther. The water was almost up to his waist.

"What if we pay you?" I asked.

Matt corrected me. "No, we can't, remember?"

"Fine," I said. "Hank can pay you."

"I can?"

"This is ridiculous," Alicia said. "Bring the boat here."

My brother's eyes bulged. He was watching the water near Bobby. Something was moving. Something large and dark. Pepedro saw it, too. But it was too large to be a caiman and too dark for a boto.

"Wait," Hank yelled. "Wait. Jack's right. I could pay you. How much do you want?"

"Money? I don't want money!" Bobby said. "I have money. What I want is a little fame, you know? I'd love to be walking through an airport one day and glance at one of those newsstands with all the magazines, and see . . . me, me, me, me. In a sharp, tight-fitting suit with a purple tie. I'd look casual, elegant, maybe a little brilliant."

Alicia interrupted. "What does this have to do with us?"

"Those battery designs will make me the greatest

inventor of the twenty-first century! I'll revolutionize transportation, and this time my father will have to admit to my brilliance!"

"We'll tell everyone you stole the designs," Ava said. "No one will believe you."

The dark shape was behind him now, circling.

"Oh, princess, don't you know anything? I'll keep you tied up in the courts for decades while I'm making billions."

Gritting her teeth, Ava snapped, "Don't call me princess."

"I'll call you what I like," Bobby said. "If you do manage to survive the jungle and return to Manaus, I'll already be gone and putting the batteries into production."

Bobby started to push away. The dark shape surfaced to his left, then swam beneath the boat. He still hadn't seen it. And maybe warning him would have been the right thing to do. But he was about to abandon us. And Matt said this species wasn't deadly. Painful, maybe. But not lethal. "Wait!" I cried.

He paused. "What? It's over. You lost."

"I'm sure we can make a deal. The battery was kind of my idea, so I have a say in this, too. How about we give you five percent?"

Hank raised his eyebrows. "Your idea, Jack?"

Alicia wagged her finger. "No, no, no. Five percent is too high," she said. "Three percent."

Bobby chuckled. "You'll get zero percent." He looked over our heads at the surrounding forest. "Assuming you even get out of this place alive. Look," he said, placing both hands on the side of the boat, preparing to jump in, "it's been real, but I have work to do."

Standing beside me, Pepedro tossed a stone into the river half a meter from Bobby's waist. Instantly, the dark shape darted toward him. The giant electric eel wrapped itself around his right leg and pumped him full of nine hundred volts. Every muscle in his body instantly tensed. His eyes bulged. His teeth clenched. For a few seconds, I thought he was going to explode. Then Bobby released his death grip on the bow of the small boat and fell face-first into the water.

18
CRIMES AGAINST THE
AMAZON

THE *VON HUMBOLDT* COMPLETED THE RETURN TRIP TO Manaus in only two days, since Hank had it drive through the night while we slept. The food was way better than on the first part of our journey. There was a freezer in the hold that none of us had known about, and it was packed with frozen fruits and vegetables. The solar-powered shower that extended from a hidden compartment was probably our favorite surprise, though. The closest thing any of us had gotten to a shower was Matt nearly getting doused by that monkey. We all needed a serious scrubbing, including Bobby, but we didn't allow him that luxury. Everyone had kind of wanted to leave him there on the riverbank, but there was no way he would've survived. So we locked him in the tiniest bunk like a prisoner.

The city appeared in the distance early Saturday evening, and Hank called for us to join him around his laptop. He was finally able to connect to the Internet, and none of us were sure how to react when we found that Cheryl had worked as planned. The satellite had been reprogrammed. She'd captured images of all the points on Hank's map, just as we'd hoped. But that also meant we had proof that Super Floor had begun its logging operations. In several photographs, sections of the jungle that were once entirely green had been stripped of their trees.

"I can't believe it," Alicia said.

Hank closed the window showing the satellite photographs. "I know it's hard to look at," he said, "but now we have proof. Now the authorities have been alerted, and they can stop them from doing any more damage. But that only stops this one operation. If we want to prevent this from happening again somewhere else in the jungle, we have to stop Dona Maria."

"To kill the snake, you must cut off the head," Pepedro said. He studied my reaction for a second before laughing. "No, no. You misunderstand me. I don't think we should actually cut off her head."

"We need to show everyone that she is behind this terrible plot," Alicia said.

"We have to find her first," Ava reminded them.

"What about her factory?" I suggested.

"I have a better idea," Hank said. He opened the tracking program he'd written for his drive. A detailed map of the city appeared on his screen, with a green bull's-eye blinking in what looked like the center of Manaus. "Joao said he was going to give it to his boss. Maybe if we find the drive, we find her."

Matt pointed to the bull's-eye. "What's there?"

"Another one of her factories?" Pepedro guessed. "Or an office building?"

Hank zoomed in.

"That's not an office building," I said. The street names were familiar. We'd driven through that neighborhood on our first day in Manaus. "That's the Opera House." The memory of Dona Maria slapping my hand flashed into my mind. I could picture her desk, the beautiful business cards, and the tickets. "She was going to opening night at the opera."

Ava grabbed the computer from Hank and started typing. "Opening night is tonight," she said. She switched to another page, then pursed her lips as she read. "According to Dona Maria's twitter feed, she's going to be there. She also tagged a few other people. I think one of them is the mayor. It looks like Joaquim is going, too."

"You think they're in on this?" I asked.

"Or maybe they just like the opera," Pepedro said.

"How are we going to get the drive back from her with all those people around?" Matt asked.

The three geniuses looked to me for an answer. Why

233

me? Well, I wasn't just the tree-climbing, window-jumping, random button pusher in our group. Hank was a world-famous inventor and scientist. Ava could build anything and learn a new language in a plane ride. Matt had more scientific knowledge in his curly-haired head than most textbooks.

All three of them were brilliant.

But I could scheme.

Down below, Bobby was knocking on his locked cabin door. I was supposed to bring him dinner and I'd totally forgotten. But my fishing buddy could wait. Holding my hands behind my back, I gazed out at the city. "I don't know exactly how we're going to get it back," I said, "but I do know one thing."

"What's that?" Hank asked.

"You and I are going to need tuxedos."

The Amazon Theatre was a quick taxi ride from where we docked the *Von Humboldt*. Our split with Bobby wasn't exactly emotional. He was just as happy to see us drive off in the cab as we were to see him walking away from the pier and out of our lives. Alicia knew of an upscale clothing store near the opera house, so after dropping Pepedro, Ava, and Matt at an electronics shop down the block, where they hoped to find a projector, she led Hank and me inside. She explained our situation in Portuguese—or our need for tuxedos, anyway. Within five minutes, we were surrounded by men in finely cut suits stretching measuring tape across our shoulders and around our waists. I tried to act unimpressed. Mature. You know, like I did this sort of thing all the time. But then this one bald guy got close to my stomach and I totally giggled. The highlight of the whole affair? They also had socks. Clean, dry, beautiful socks that made my jungle-soaked feet want to dance.

I found a new pair of high-tops in a sports store on the same block, and when Hank and I hurried to the park across the street from the famous theater, my siblings and the boy with the million dollar foot were waiting for us.

Hank adjusted my bow tie. "You look sharp," he said.

His tie was slightly crooked, but I didn't say anything. I checked my part.

235

"Your hair's fine, Jack," Ava said, "and I still don't see why I don't get to go."

"I told you," I said. "One kid and one adult is fine. Two kids going in on their own? That would be suspicious. Plus you're playing a super important role. Did you get what you need?"

"Pretty much," Matt said.

"We'll be fine," Ava added. "Are you ready?"

"We're ready," Hank said.

"Should we huddle or something?" Pepedro asked.

Scientists don't huddle. Or not usually, anyway. But Hank threw one arm around my back and the other around Ava's shoulders. Everyone else linked up, too. "What now?" Hank asked. "What does a soccer team do?"

"If we were a team," Pepedro said, "we would be the strangest team in the world."

"The world? We're grander than that," Hank said. "Here's to the strangest team in the universe! Or maybe our solar system, anyway."

Our huddle broke, and the six of us left the cover of the trees and crossed the street to the front of the theater. The faded pink-and-white building could have been a palace. Wide stone steps curved up from the street toward the entrance. The rows of columns and stone arches belonged on a royal castle, and although we couldn't see it from where we stood, I remembered reading that the domed roof was equally epic, covered with something like thirty-six thousand colored tiles arranged to resemble the Brazilian flag.

"Wow," Matt said.

"Exactly," Hank added.

The opera had already begun, but the first act was scheduled to end in a few minutes. Before the start of the second act, there was a half-hour intermission. Alicia said many operagoers would step outside, either to smoke or to check the score of a big soccer match taking place that evening. That was when we'd slip into the theater.

"How do you know so much?" Ava asked.

"Sometimes I sneak in," Alicia admitted.

Hank and I approached the front entrance, with Alicia a few steps behind. The doors to the grand theater swung open, and a few dozen operagoers rushed outside, reaching for their cigarettes, cigars, and phones. We stood behind one of the thirty-foot-tall marble columns, waiting for the crowd to spread out. The smell of smoke was revolting, but I tried not to cough. As a middle schooler in a tuxedo, I stood out enough already.

Behind us, I could see Alicia studying the operagoers.

"What are you looking for?" I asked.

A man with long, curly gray hair shouted as he stared at his phone. He turned it around to show another tuxedoed gentleman. The second man tilted his head back and screamed at the sky. "I'm looking for passionate soccer fans," she explained, "and those two are perfect."

Alicia walked over to the pair. At first they didn't even look up from the gray-haired man's phone. Then she handed each one of them a small card of some kind. Both of them smiled like little kids. Alicia held up two fingers and the men reached into the pockets of their tuxedoes and each

237

produced a ticket. She took the tickets, bowed in thanks, then pointed down toward the street. The two men hurried off at a jog, and our clever friend walked back with two tickets to the opera.

"What just happened?" I asked.

"There's a very important match tonight," she said. "No true fan of football would want to be inside the Opera House. I gave them autographed photos of Pepedro and told them where they should go to watch the game." She handed us the small slips of paper. "And now you have tickets."

At the entrance, the usher glared at me but let us through. Inside, faded yellow light glowed from chandeliers. A stone balcony curved around the outside of the room, held up by more columns. The floor was polished marble and shiny enough to catch my reflection. Ava was right. My hair looked fine.

"Enough stargazing, Jack," Hank said, tugging the elbow of my tuxedo jacket. We crossed the room and he pointed overhead, to a painting of gods and angels that stretched across the ceiling. "They brought the artist over from Europe to create that mural," he said. Then he looked out into the crowd. "I don't see Dona Maria."

Hank had loaded his tracking program onto a phone, then given it to me to use. I pulled it out of my pocket and opened the app. An usher approached and spoke in Portuguese. Once he realized neither of us understood him, he tapped my phone, then shook his finger. I pocketed it.

"Let's hope she's still here," I said to Hank.

The theater itself was four stories tall. Giant curtains painted with a river scene hid the stage from view. A few hundred seats were spaced across the floor in front of the stage, and the rest were spread out among the small private booths that wrapped around the inside. As Hank and I walked down the center aisle, I scanned the seats on the floor, then looked up to the second level. A pair of wrinkled hands gripped the railing in a booth near the stage. Then Dona Maria leaned forward, watching the crowd. Joaquim, the chef and owner from Saudade, sat on her left. Behind them, Joao was leaning against the wall with his arms crossed. The mayor of Manaus stood to Dona Maria's right, talking to two other men.

I continued down the center aisle.

No one stopped me.

I placed my hands on the wooden stage and jumped up.

Still no one held me back.

Then I turned and stood facing the growing crowd with my back to the giant curtains. My heart was beating faster by the second. I felt like someone was stepping on my chest. A light flickered on the highest balcony at the back of the

239

room. Hopefully that meant my siblings and Pepedro were on schedule.

Hank joined me on the stage. I glanced up at Dona Maria. She hadn't moved, but she was watching me like a hawk eyeing its next meal. I gulped.

"Ladies and gent—" My voice cracked. I coughed and tried again. "Ladies and gentlemen," I shouted. The chatter and conversation stopped as the audience focused on the stage. "Before we begin the second act, I have an important announcement to make. We have a criminal in the audience. A liar and a thief."

Several people gasped.

"I told you we wouldn't need a translator," Hank whispered. "Sorry, keep going. You're doing great."

The empty seats were quickly disappearing. Three ushers were hurrying down the center aisle. I held out my hands and shouted, "Wait!"

The ushers came closer.

Up in Dona Maria's booth, Joaquim leaned over the railing and yelled in Portuguese. The ushers stopped. He waved his hands and pointed at me as he spoke. A few people in the crowd were looking at me and nodding in approval. I waited.

Joaquim cupped his hands around his mouth. "I told them to listen," he said. "So, go ahead. Speak!"

And so I did. My voice cracked a few more times. I kind of blabbered a little, and I probably should have rehearsed my speech, or at least written a few things down. But I managed to blurt out everything we'd discovered about Dona Maria and what she was doing to the precious rainforest. At one point, a man in the front row raised his hand. I hadn't expected that, so I called on him. He stood. "Is this part of the opera?" he asked.

"No, this is real," I said. "Super Andar, or Super Floor—they're illegally logging a huge section of the rainforest. And the woman in charge of it all is sitting right there."

I pointed. The mayor scooted away.

Finally, Dona Maria stood. "You have no proof!" she yelled. "These are lies! Lies, lies, lies. Please, someone get these crazy people off the stage so we can go on with the opera."

"Oh, but we do have proof," Hank said.

The two of us moved to the end of the stage as my siblings and our two Brazilian friends switched on a projector at the back of the room, covering the curtain with multicolored light.

As their slide show of Cheryl's images appeared on the backdrop behind us, Hank began narrating. "This is what the jungle looked like two days ago," Hank said, pointing to a green swath of the forest. "And this," he said as the next image appeared, "is what it looks like right now, after Super Andar did its work."

Several people in the audience gasped. Others shouted up at Dona Maria in her booth. The mayor was shifting away from the old woman, and it looked like Joaquim was firing questions at her. But Dona Maria was staring only at us. Hank was finished. And although I hadn't planned out my speech, I did know how I was going to wrap it up. I pulled my notebook out of my jacket pocket and studied her name one last time before staring up at her. "Dona Maria Aparecida Oliveiros Dos Santos," I announced, "you are guilty of crimes against the Amazon rainforest and plain, old-fashioned theft. I demand that you and your loggers never return to the jungle and that you give us back what is rightfully ours!"

The theater was silent.

Against the wall, Joao was sliding closer to the booth's exit. Joaquim pressed his hand to his heart, then began to clap. A few others followed. I kind of wanted the applause to spread the way it does in the movies. I'm not sure how that would've helped us get the drive back, but I liked the idea of being onstage, in a sweet new tuxedo, as seven hundred people in fancy clothes cheered.

Unfortunately, Dona Maria killed my moment.

Pleading with the other guests, Dona Maria pointed to

me, then placed her hands on her chest. Clearly, she was begging them to believe her. And it didn't look like it was working. She moved to the edge of the railing, lifted her cane, and yelled, *"Mentiroso! Intrujão!"*

One of the ushers hurried to the edge of the stage. "She's calling you a liar and a thief," he explained.

I was expecting her to yell at me again, call the images fakes, maybe even demand my arrest. Instead, Joao held open the door as the old woman spun around, crouched low, and sped out of her private booth in her rocket-powered shoes.

This was not part of our plan. She was supposed to confess. Maybe even cry. "What now?" I asked.

"I guess we chase her," Hank said.

The two of us jumped to the carpeted floor and sprinted up the center aisle as the ushers stepped aside. We burst into the lobby just as she was descending the last few steps of the winding marble stairway. Joao was at her side.

Hank and I blocked the nearest exit as Matt, Ava, Alicia, and Pepedro hurried down the stairway on the other side of the room. A balcony wrapped around the room on the second level, and Joaquim and the mayor appeared at the railing.

"Give us back the drive," I said.

On the balcony, Joaquim yelled down. "Return the inventions!"

The mayor, standing next to him, applauded.

Curious operagoers began crowding into the lobby.

Pointing her cane at the balcony, Dona Maria said, "You support them? You support the Americans?"

"We support what is right," the mayor replied. "No one who cuts down our precious rainforest deserves to be called a Brazilian."

The operagoers cheered.

My siblings and the others were standing beside us now. Joao was scowling at me. I moved behind Matt.

"Give us the drive," Ava said.

A woman in a long sequined dress added, "Give them what is theirs!"

Dona Maria edged forward, away from the steps. "So much trouble over such a little gadget," she said, pulling the drive out of her purse. She twirled the tiny device in her crooked fingers. "Fascinating piece of technology. Joao and I were very impressed. Impossible to copy. And you are here, so I imagine you can track its location, too?"

"Down to the square meter," Hank said.

Forty or fifty operagoers had now moved into the lobby. A dozen or two more had spread out along the balcony.

The old woman eyed the device again. "How did you get the pictures if we control the satellite?"

"We have another satellite," Ava answered.

Dona Maria turned to Hank. "You have two satellites?"

"No," I said, "the second one belongs to them."

Joao held his hands together, pleading. "Dona Maria, I didn't know—"

"Quiet! You were supposed to be so brilliant, and yet some children outsmarted you? I'm very disappointed, Joao. And as for the rest of you, well, you are all very clever. I've been told the designs stored in this little box could be worth hundreds of millions of dollars. Maybe more."

"They're not your ideas," I reminded her.

"Yes, they are," Dona Maria said. "They belong to me, and I am going to take this drive with me." She glared up at the mayor and Joaquim. "Somewhere people appreciate my talents. Joao, let's get out of here!"

Her bleached-blond assistant moved toward us, then stopped. Sure, he was skinny, but I was still surprised. Normally we don't inspire much fear in people, from a physical standpoint. Then I heard a noise behind me.

Four large operagoers blocked the doors.

Joao shouted something in Portuguese and darted for an exit on the opposite side. As Dona Maria crouched down, he burst out through the doors and escaped. The old crook cruised after him, then slowed. Before she reached the swinging door, she lurched. The four men were now hurrying to block the other exits. Panicked, she stomped

245

her cane down on the marble floor. Then she slammed the heels of her battery-powered boots three times and crouched again, ready to race away. But Dona Maria wasn't going anywhere. She was mumbling angrily in Portuguese.

Alicia and Pepedro both began to laugh.

"What is it?" I asked. "What's so funny?"

"She says the batteries in her boots are dead," Pepedro said.

"The drive," Ava said, holding out her hand.

Dona Maria reluctantly dug through her purse, removed the familiar drive, and flicked it into the air over Hank's head. The inventor wasn't quick enough to snag it. But my brother lunged back and snatched the precious device out of the air before it could fall onto the hard floor.

"How did you grab that?" I asked. "You can't even catch a basketball!"

Matt winked. "I don't care about basketballs," he said. Gently, he tapped the drive and added, "I care about ideas."

Dona Maria continued muttering in her native language. "She's saying something about how she should have retired to some island," Ava said. "Flo-something?"

"Florida?" I asked.

"No, Florianópolis," Pepedro explained. "Very nice place. It's like the Hawaii of Brazil."

The operagoers applauded. I bowed.

247

"We're bowing?" Matt said. "Really?"

Pepedro joined me, then Hank. Eventually my siblings gave in, too. We stopped only when the mayor approached with Joaquim at her side.

"What do you want?" Dona Maria asked. "Are you going to try to arrest me for chopping down some trees?"

"Not today," the mayor answered. "I don't know when it will happen, but everyone will know what you have done, Dona Maria. You will be punished for your crimes against the Amazon."

The old woman had no response. She turned her back to us and staggered out through the exit on her powerless shoes. And look, I know that watching a crooked business-woman shuffle away on battery-powered boots should not have been sad. She was a despicable person. A cheater. A liar. And yet part of me felt bad for Dona Maria as she left all alone.

Alicia placed her hand on my shoulder. "Don't shed a tear for her," she said. "She might be in some trouble now, but she is still very rich."

My sympathy vanished.

As the crowd started to return to the theater, we thanked the mayor and Joaquim for listening. Then Hank spoke privately with Alicia and Pepedro before tapping his watch and announcing that we were late for an appointment.

"An appointment?" Matt asked. "What do you mean?"

"We're not going to the dentist or something, are we?" I asked, joking.

"People do that, you know," Ava pointed out. "It's called 'dental tourism.'"

"Wait, seriously? Are we going to the dentist?"

Hank laughed but refused to explain what appointment he was talking about. He hurried us down to the avenue. A new limo, parked at an angle, waited at the curb.

Arms crossed, shaking her head, Ava stopped at the bottom of the steps. "We're not getting in another limo. No way."

"This one does look a little nicer," Pepedro said.

The driver stepped around the front of the car and opened the doors. As Hank convinced my siblings that we were not in danger, I jumped in back and searched the icebox. Pepedro and Alicia slid in as well. A few frigid cans of Guarana were waiting for us. The seats were dark  leather and as soft as couches. I kicked back, sipped the strange soda, and decided I wanted to remain in the limo for the rest of our trip to Brazil. The others could tour the sites. They could visit museums or go out to restaurants. I was going to remain in air-conditioned luxury, eating takeout and sipping ice-cold soft drinks.

Matt climbed in next, then Ava. Settling back into the cushioned leather, I was starting to think about how I could redesign my bedroom to be more like a limo when Hank popped his head in. "Jack," he said, "would you mind riding up front with me? There's something I want to talk to you about."

My siblings and the Brazilians all watched me. I hesitated. This didn't feel like the right time to split from them, even if I was just going up to the front seat. But Matt told me to go, and Ava agreed. Sitting between Hank and the driver was a little awkward, even if the car was huge, but I got over it and talked to Hank about a whole bunch of things. The coming school year, our money problems, even girls.

Hank said he might have a solution to our financial concerns. I perked up. "You do?" I asked.

"Yes, but first I have a confession, Jack," he said.

The road was winding through open country now, sloping down a hill toward what looked like an airfield.

"A confession? What did you do?"

"The battery idea . . . it didn't really work."

"What do you mean?"

"I mean the battery I've been working on, based on your

idea with the eels. It's fine. It's okay. But it's not much better than what's out there already."

My heart sank. "Then why did we just go to all that trouble to get the drive back?"

"Well, she stole the codes to my satellite, for one," Hank said. "The other designs might be worth something, too. The Taser, for instance. And I'm not saying the eel-inspired battery application is totally dead. Not at all. I think there are a number of lessons to learn from how these giant eels store energy, too. There could still be some tremendous applications."

"But?"

"But there was one other thing." Hank reached over into his fanny pack, pulled out an Odoraser, and tossed it to me. "Wasn't this your idea, too?"

251

Normally, I remember my best brainstorms. "I don't know," I admitted. "Was it?"

"Sure," Hank said. "You were messing around with the nose vacuum one day, and you said something about how it would be great to have one for . . . gaseous emissions."

I chuckled. Hank hated the word I would've used. But was that really my idea? I searched my brain and, even though he was imaginary, asked the little harmonica player for help. A memory of the moment flashed back to me. "Wait, we'd just eaten burritos, right? And I was ripping some huge—"

"Yes, yes, exactly," Hank said, cutting me off before I pronounced the word. "Anyway, a friend of mine is very interested in this device. Someone you might remember."

The limo slowed as we drove through an open gate in a chain metal fence. The small airfield stretched out in front of us. Waiting on the runway was a beautiful private jet. A very beautiful and very familiar private jet. A ramp stretched down from the entrance, and a man in a cushioned armchair was rolling away from the plane in our direction.

"Uh, Hank, who is that?" I asked.

The Plexiglas partition opened behind me. Everyone was staring ahead.

"That, Jack, is Mr. J. F. Clutterbuck," Hank explained, "the billionaire inventor of the odorless sock."

"Why is he in a drivable chair?" Ava asked.

"He is very, very lazy. Now, as you know, Jack, Mr. Clutterbuck is in the odor business." The limousine stopped. "Jack inspired me to engineer the Odoraser," Hank explained, "and our friend Mr. Clutterbuck is interested in buying it."

Alicia slapped her hand down on the top of my seat. "Ten million dollars!" she exclaimed. "Jack will take nothing less!"

I smiled. A million or two would've been just fine.

19
OUT OF THE DUMPSTER

OKAY, SO ALICIA'S GOAL WAS A LITTLE OVERAMBITIOUS. Mine, too. Clutterbuck wasn't there to write me a check for that much cash. But Alicia practiced her negotiation skills on the billionaire, and Clutterbuck agreed to pay Hank and me a decent amount of money for the rights to the Odoraser. Enough to pay off our bills and cover the next year of rent, anyway. And Clutterbuck said that if his engineers perfected the device and he started to sell it, we'd share in the profits.

That was the good news. The bad news was that he didn't give us a ride home in his jet. He was on vacation, on his way to Florianópolis—the island Dona Maria had mentioned. He happened to be flying south when Hank had e-mailed him from the boat, so he stopped in Manaus to refuel. After we'd negotiated, I asked if we could join him for the island vacation.

Sadly, he laughed.

For the next few days, we recuperated in our hotel—a

much nicer one, thanks to Hank—and toured the city with Pepedro and Alicia. Most of the time, Pepedro wore a hat pulled low, so people wouldn't stop him for selfies. We also had another surprise guest. On the morning after our return to Manaus, we were limping downstairs for breakfast when Min walked through the hotel's front doors. Hank froze. Whether they were an item or not, they probably wanted a moment. But we didn't let them have it. I charged forward ahead of my siblings and wrapped my arms around her. Min was rigid as a sculpture at first. None of us really ever hug. Or not like that, anyway. But she softened, returned the embrace, then wrapped my siblings in quick hugs before Hank unfroze and tried to explain himself. We left them in the lobby and went into the restaurant for breakfast. Over the next few days, I shattered my cheese-bread-eating record and changed my socks about four times daily, just because I could, and when it was time for us to leave Brazil, Alicia and Pepedro wouldn't stand for any emotional good-byes. Plus Hank promised to buy them tickets to visit us in New York over the holidays. Whether it was true or not, we all promised that we'd see one another soon.

Once we were back home in New York, I wanted to head straight for the apartment, lock myself in my room, and play video games for a week. But the others insisted on going straight from the airport to the lab. Hank and Min stayed with us, and he was nervous about his beloved headquarters, even though she assured him she'd hired a great cleaning crew. Not only that, but she'd also made a deal with Bobby to pay for the effort. He funded the cleanup and deposited a bunch of money in some kind of trust account for our education, and in return, Hank agreed not to press charges against him.

A car dropped us off at the end of the block, and we followed Hank to the Dumpster. He was about to press the button when the lid popped open.

A man and a woman stood up.

The five of us nearly leaped back across the street.

The man was bearded, with huge, round eyes. A pair of pens stuck out of the pocket of his Hawaiian shirt. The woman had pale skin, thin glasses, and blond hair with black roots. An old newspaper was stuck to the back of her blouse. She peeled it off and extended her hand. "Hello, Hank," she said. "I'm not sure if you remember me, but I'm Elise Crowell, of the NASA Office of Technology. We've met before. This is my colleague, Marvin Miller."

Hank reached into the Dumpster and shook their hands. "Hello," he said. He drew the word out, so it was almost more of a question than a greeting. "Can I help you?"

The man was looking at me and smiling. His eyes were familiar. And the beard, too. "The plane!" I said.

255

"What are you talking about, Jack?" Ava asked.

I started to point at the man, but Hank knocked my hand down. He says it's rude to point. "You were on the plane to Manaus, weren't you? You gave me the earplugs!"

Miller nodded. "Did they work?"

"Perfectly," I said. Then I remembered our conversation. "I don't get it. You had an accent. I assumed you were Brazilian."

"No, I'm just good with accents," he said. "Want to hear my Irish brogue?"

"Please don't," Ava said. "We've had enough fake accents."

"Hank, you are a difficult man to find," Crowell said, climbing out of the Dumpster. Matt stepped forward to help her, but she pushed his hand away. "And you kids are difficult to follow."

Ava's head snapped back slightly. "You were following us?"

I squinted at the woman. That morning we'd walked into the ruined lab seemed like years ago. But now I recognized her from that day. The pair of them had been standing across the street after we'd chased Bobby out of the lab. They were eating popsicles. How long had they been watching us?

Miller climbed out of the Dumpster and stared down at a green stain on his khaki pants, then shrugged. "We tracked you for a while in Brazil, too, but we lost you in the city."

Neither Matt nor Ava said a word. Hank stood between us and the odd pair. They didn't seem dangerous. Just weird. But I didn't mind that Hank was being protective.

"The NASA Office of Technology?" he said. "I don't think I've heard of that."

"We go by NOT," Crowell said.

"And we're sort of secret," Miller added.

"So you're the Secret NASA Office of Technology?" I asked.

"Yes," she said, "I suppose so."

I tried not to laugh. The geniuses needed a few seconds to get the joke. Miller and Crowell needed even longer.

"You're SNOT," Ava said.

"No, we're NOT," Miller corrected her.

I could've gone on like that for at least five more minutes, but Hank was getting impatient. "SNOT or NOT," Hank said, "I'd like you to explain why you've been following them and what you're doing in my Dumpster."

Miller looked to Crowell to answer. "We need your help," she said. "NASA needs your help."

"With what?" Ava asked.

"I can't tell you here," Crowell replied. "This is highly sensitive information, but we are wondering if you would be interested in going on an undercover mission of sorts."

"A mission?" Matt asked. "To where?"

257

"They need rest," Min insisted.

"Unless it's somewhere really awesome," Ava said.

"Can we go back to Hawaii?" I asked.

"We can't tell you where you'd be going," Miller said. "Not here, anyway."

"I'm sorry," Hank said, "but the children and I are planning to stick together for a while. Any trips I take, they will have to come, too." He glanced at Min. "My friend here, too."

Miller nodded. "That's great, actually. You see, we need the children to join you. This is a very unusual assignment. We need a group of highly intelligent individuals, and we need them to impersonate a family."

258

"That shouldn't be a problem," Hank said.

"No?" Crowell asked. "Why not?"

Hank glanced back at each of us in turn. "Because we are a family."

Then he reached forward, pressed the button that activates the Dumpster, and invited the scientists down to the lab so we could learn more. I let the others go first. Min started questioning Crowell. Matt and Ava were theorizing about what this strange mission might involve. Ava wasn't totally sure she wanted to go anywhere at all. I figured Matt would have the same attitude. His college classes would be starting up again soon, and I assumed he'd want to spend the next few weeks studying in preparation. But he actually seemed really excited about another adventure. As for me? Well, I was tired. Exhausted, really. My body was aching. My feet were still a wreck. The welts all over my skin had barely faded. My stomach needed at least a few weeks to recover from all that cheese bread. But as we walked down toward the lab, I found myself smiling. I didn't care where this next adventure might take us or even what it would involve. We were a family. A strange, mismatched mix of individuals, but still a family.

I'd follow the geniuses anywhere.

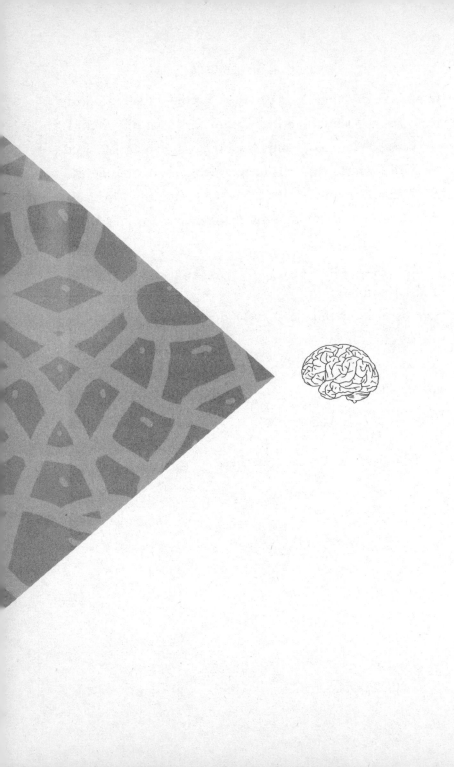

TWELVE MOSTLY ESSENTIAL QUESTIONS ABOUT *LOST IN THE JUNGLE*

ANTARCTICA, THE FOCUS OF *AT THE BOTTOM OF THE World*, the first book in the Jack and the Genuises series, is a pretty amazing place. The deep ocean is equally astounding, and that's part of the reason we sent the crew to Hawaii in *Jack and the Geniuses: In the Deep Blue Sea*. The setting of *Lost in the Jungle*, the Amazon rainforest, ranks right up there as one of the most spectacular and scientifically fascinating spots on our planet. It hosts 25 percent of the world's species and accounts for 15 percent of the photosynthesis happening on the surface. The facts that Jack and the kids relay about the rainforest and its many incredible creatures aren't made up. This is real science, and we're sure you still have some questions about the Amazon, the incredible technology the geniuses use, and the very unusual behaviors of sloths.

So here are a few questions and answers about Jack and the geniuses and their journey through the jungle.

I. ARE CUBESATS REAL? Absolutely. They're small enough

to hold in your hands and capable of capturing images, receiving and transmitting radio signals, and carrying out scientific experiments. In 2015, as CEO of the Planetary Society, Bill helped launch a slightly larger version of a CubeSat, LightSail 1, and the group is planning to send a second model into space in 2018. Both LightSail satellites are designed to deploy solar sails.

2. WAIT. WHAT'S A SOLAR SAIL? You don't know? Join the Planetary Society! In the meantime, we'll explain. Instead of molecules of air in the wind pushing a sail and thrusting a boat through the water, a spacecraft with solar sails gets pushed through space by light from the Sun. Light is made of particles of energy we call "photons." Even though they have no mass or weight, they have momentum. When they bounce off the sails, each photon gives the spacecraft a tiny push. And unlike a rocket, a solar sail never runs out of fuel. Solar sails may one day carry spacecraft all over the Solar System.

3. BACK TO THOSE CUBESATS . . . COULD KIDS REALLY BUILD ONE? Yes! Students at the St. Thomas More Cathedral School, an elementary school in Arlington, Virginia, worked together to design, build, and even launch their own CubeSat—with a little help from NASA. (Not the SNOT division, though.) Sure, there were more kids involved, and they took more time than Ava and Matt, but they prove that it's possible. Their satellite, the STMSat-1, cruised into orbit on May 16, 2016. And just like Cheryl, the STMSat-1 photographs the planet from above and then sends these images down to the ground.

4. IS THE AMAZON JUNGLE ACTUALLY IN TROUBLE? Brazil's National Institute for Space Research (INPE) uses satellite images to track deforestation, or the loss of rainforest land to logging, mining, and other human-led and naturally occuring processes. For the year ending in July 2016, the Brazilian portion of the Amazon lost an area nearly three times the size of the state of Rhode Island to deforestation. So, yeah, we've got a problem.

Indeed, forests all over the planet are disappearing. And logging isn't the only cause. Mining for natural resources, building new roads, clearing land for farms and livestock, plus natural change—all these forces conspire to shrink the tree-covered portions of our planet.

5. DOES THIS IMPACT CLIMATE CHANGE? Very much so. Greenhouse gas emissions fill the air with carbon dioxide, trapping heat near Earth's surface and warming the planet. Deforestation contributes more greenhouse gas emissions than gasoline-burning cars and trucks. While we can't necessarily stop forests from shrinking due to natural processes, we can work to prevent humans from unnecessarily destroying our tree-covered landscapes by supporting organizations that fight deforestation.

263

6. DO SCIENTISTS USE SATELLITES TO MONITOR THE RAIN FOREST, THE WAY JACK AND THE GENIUSES DO IN THE STORY? Well, besides government agencies like INPE, scientists and private citizens are focusing on the problem. Planet, a company that operates a fleet of more than a hundred miniature satellites, hopes to have enough of the spacecraft in orbit to image every spot on Earth at least once a day. Among other things, these images could help governments and organizations discover illegal logging or deforestation operations in the Amazon rainforest. The company now generates more images than people could possibly scan, so Planet launched a competition to encourage software developers to design programs that can automatically find changes in the landscape. It's the kind of thing that Ava and Matt would probably enter.

7. JACK USES CHERYL TO SURF THE WEB. COULD CUBESATS REALLY PROVIDE INTERNET ACCESS? Bill here. I'd love to see every person on the planet have access to three things: clean drinking water; clean, renewable sources of electricity; and unlimited, unfiltered information. That last one usually means the Internet, but half the world still doesn't have reliable, high-speed access to the Web. Global access to information is essential. No matter where you are on the planet, you should be able to get online, the way Jack does in the story. Luckily, a number of groups are working on that, and their approaches won't require the climbing of absurdly tall trees. For example, a company called OneWeb wants to launch a fleet of nine hundred satellites capable of providing Internet access to the entire planet by 2027.

8. OKAY, ENOUGH ABOUT SATELLITES. ON PAGE 40, THE TAXI DRIVER INSISTS THAT A BRAZILIAN NAMED ALBERTO SANTOS-DUMONT INVENTED FLIGHT, NOT THE WRIGHT BROTHERS. WHO WAS HE? Santos-Dumont, the son of a wealthy coffee-producing family, is an important figure in the history of aviation. At first, he built and flew hot-air balloons and blimps. He studied and lived in Paris and often anchored his dirigible to a streetlamp outside his apartment, then flew it around the city as his own personal air taxi. But his first official flight in an airplane-type craft—known as heavier-than-air flight—was in 1906. That's a few years after the Wright brothers' historic 1903 success, and subsequent succesful flights completed before 1906. That's our take. But we wouldn't advise arguing this point with a Brazilian.

9. IS BETSY REAL? We based Betsy on an actual device, the Atlas Powered Ascender (APA), which can whisk two people up to the height of a thirty-story building in only thirty seconds. The device was invented by a bunch of big kids—students at the Massachusetts Institute of Technology—but it would be tough for Ava to lug through the jungle, since it weighs twenty-two pounds. Oh, and it doesn't actually feature a wrist-mounted crossbow. But Greg once interviewed a guy who built one of those in his apartment—you know, for fun—and we thought it would be cool to add to Ava's invention.

10. WHY DO SLOTHS CLIMB DOWN TO THE FOREST FLOOR TO DO THEIR WEEKLY BUSINESS? Ah, yes. The most important question of all. Scientists have been puzzling over this for years. Some speculate that it helps the trees. Others have proposed that it gives the sloths a chance to socialize. "Hey, dude, meet you on the forest floor in three hours, okay?"

Recently, a group of mammalian ecologists at the University of Wisconsin–Madison studied fourteen two-toed sloths to find a possible explanation. They found that when the sloths climb down to the ground and, um, drop off their package, moths living in their fur slip out and lay eggs in the droppings. Usually, a few eggs in preexisting droppings scattered around the area have hatched by that point, and these newborn moths fly up and snuggle into the sloth's fur. So what's in it for the preguiça? The researchers discovered that the moths encourage the growth of algae in the sloth's fur and that these algae can be a great source of nutrients for the slow-moving creatures. So they're guaranteeing themselves a good snack.

Of course, the sloths aren't the only amazing creatures Jack and the geniuses come across or panic about in the story.

Botos, Brazilian free-tailed bats, golden lancehead snakes, piranhas, jaguars, caimans, and all manner of insects—we'd have to write another book to detail them all. So here's an idea instead: do some research of your own and see what you can find out. Who knows, maybe you'll be inspired to travel to the rainforest and discover some species of your own one day!

11. WAIT, SO MOTHS LIVE IN THEIR FUR, TOO—NOT JUST BEETLES? Yep. Plus bacteria, fungi, and other creatures. It's a real party. And we're glad we're not invited.

12. IS ELECTROPHORUS ELECTRICUS MAGNUS A REAL CREATURE? No, but *Electrophorus electricus* is the scientific name for the electric eel. And electric eels are very real inhabitants of the Amazon basin and other areas. Plus, they're not really eels. They're actually a species of knifefish. Anyway, we consulted with James Albert, a biologist and electric eel expert at the University of Louisiana at Lafayette, who noted that all living things create electricity. Humans included. "What makes electric fish so cool is that they can control the electricity," he said. They can emit weak electric fields to find prey in murky waters or stronger ones to shock curious scientists. In late 2017, Vanderbilt University neurobiologist Ken Catania described an experiment in which a one-foot-long electric eel leaped out of its holding tank to strike him in the arm when he reached into the water. The shock he

267

received wasn't too painful, but Catania estimated that a large eel would be capable of delivering a jolt stronger than a police Taser.

So remember, kids: never pet an electric eel.

GROWTH IN THE RAINFOREST—AN EXPERIMENT BY BILL NYE

ONE OF THE SURPRISING FEATURES OF THE RAINFOREST IS that it's not all thick vegetation and growth. Near riverbanks and on hillsides, you might find the kind of thick, tangled plants and bushes that Jack and the crew hack through on their way to find Hank. But in the depths of the rainforest, beneath the canopy, the forest floor isn't so crowded with vegetation.

Why? I'm glad you asked! It's all about the light. Plants need sunlight to thrive, and the canopy—the thick layer of intertwined treetops—swallows up most of the sunlight striking the region, preventing light from penetrating down to the ground.

Here's an experiment you can conduct at home to see the difference.

MATERIALS

Seeds (I'm kooky for cabbage seeds, but any kind will do)

Potting soil

Two small flowerpots or paper cups

A table

A lamp

Three books (the Jack and the Geniuses series works best)

A recyclable plastic bag

STEPS

1. Plant the seeds in two separate pots or cups packed with potting soil.

2. Read the books, then place them in the plastic bag and set them on the table.

3. Place one cup on top of the books and under the lamp. The stack moves the seeds a little closer to the light.

4. Measure the cup's distance from the lamp—fifteen centimeters (about six inches) is good.

5. Place the other pot/cup under the table, so that it's not directly under the lamplight.

6. Measure the distance of the cup from the lamp—150 centimeters (about sixty inches) is ideal.

7. Keep the soil damp but not soggy.

8. Watch the plants grow.

In only a week or two, you should be able to see the difference light makes and why the rainforest canopy thrives, while the light-deprived plants on the forest floor struggle to survive. After the experiment, give the plants under the table some light. They deserve it.

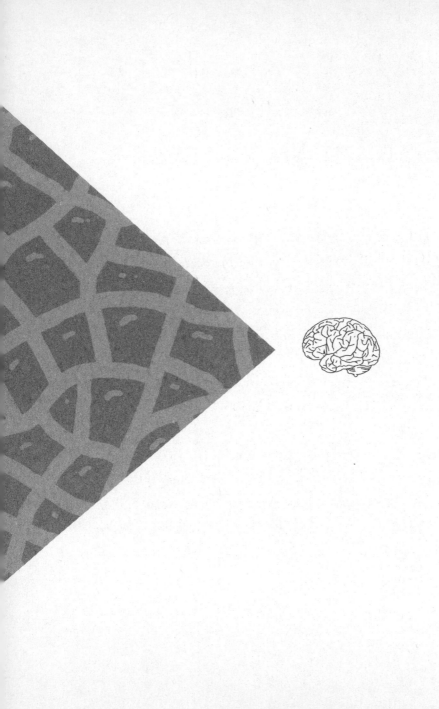

ABOUT THE AUTHORS

BILL NYE IS A SCIENCE EDUCATOR, mechanical engineer, CEO of The Planetary Society, television host, and *New York Times* bestselling author with a mission: to help foster a scientifically literate society and help people everywhere understand and appreciate the science that makes our world work. Nye is best known for his Emmy Award–winning children's show, *Bill Nye the Science Guy*, and for his new Netflix series, *Bill Nye Saves the World*. As a trusted science educator, Nye has appeared on numerous television programs, including *Good Morning America*, CNN's *New Day*, *Late Night with Seth Meyers*, *Last Week Tonight with John Oliver*, and *Real Time with Bill Maher*. He currently splits his time between New York City and Los Angeles. Follow him online at billnye.com.

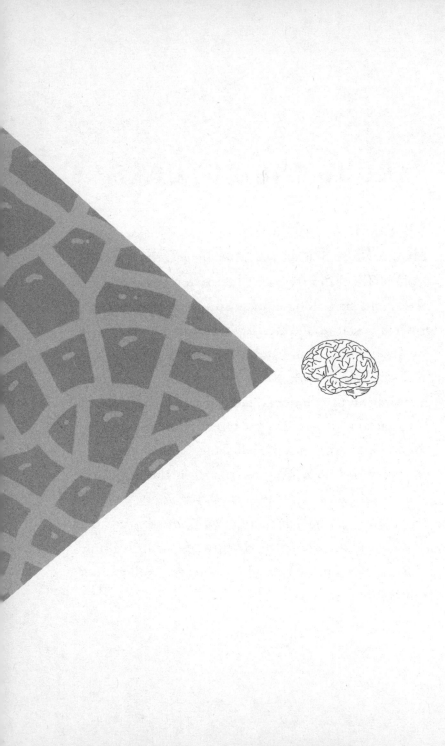

GREGORY MONE IS A NOVELIST and science writer. He has authored several children's adventure novels, including *Fish* and *Dangerous Waters: An Adventure on the Titanic*, and as a contributing editor for *Popular Science* magazine, he has written about robotics, artificial intelligence, and menacing asteroids. He lives on Martha's Vineyard, in Massachusetts, with his family. Follow him online at gregorymone.com.

IN CASE YOU MISSED IT